Wergild

Wergild
A Heartwarming Tale of Coldblooded Vengeance

Boris L. Slocum

2019

Copyright © 2019 by Boris L. Slocum

All rights reserved. No part of this publication may be reproduced, distributed, or transmitted in any form or by any means, including photocopying, recording, or other electronic or mechanical methods, without the prior written permission of the publisher, except in the case of brief quotations embodied in critical reviews and certain other noncommercial uses permitted by copyright law.

Printed in the United States of America

First Printing, 2019
Second Printing, 2023

ISBN 978-1-7335425-0-0

3B Independent Publishers
347 W. Franklin Street
Paxton, Illinois 60957

Part I
The County of Blenheim

Deirdre didn't recognize what it was at first. It was early morning, and that rumpled thing down the path looked like nothing more than a pile of trash or a hamper-load of soiled linens the felons had dumped in the road the night before. The Gheet forever were doing such things to torment — or simply because they could. And why not? There was no one to stop them. It was only when she drew close that she realized the truth of what she saw and began to scream.

It was a screaming that one way or the other, inside or out, would be with her for the rest of her life.

Wergild

The Fiend

They buried her sister Fiona three days later, two days later than custom and religion said they must. The men had their mewling and other such craven bleating to attend. Men? If they could be called that. Even now, every pious and decent one of them sat before the shroud that contained her dear sister's broken and lifeless husk, being preached at about the Walking God, the god who lived amongst them, by an asinine ape of a preacher the Gheet had insisted they hire.

Deirdre hardly could stand it. The stone of the church strangled and smothered her, the cloy and meaningless words of the minister choked her, and the filthy complacency of their so-called friends and family ... *her own family*. She couldn't breathe. Knowing what was beneath that shroud, she couldn't breathe. Every shuffle, every cough, every impatient voice-clearing was a profanity. The senseless droning of a feckless, treasonous minister was a heresy.

What use were such words? No one had done *anything*.

She couldn't breathe.

The neutered and spineless township trustees had boasted they'd gone to the local Gheet baron, and afterward they'd bragged of having been awarded wergild. In truth, they'd left the baron's keep with three ducats, the price of a sheep, no doubt grateful they'd quit the place without a swift kick in the pants, the usual reward for troubling his lordship with "idle gossip" of rape and murder. Not even shame had kept the township worthies from crowing it was the price of a *prize* sheep. Her sister. Her sister. Her best friend. *A sheep*.

She couldn't breathe.

Twice her mother had reached for her hand from where she sat in the pew next to her, hoping to calm Deirdre and to settle her writhing and twisting. *What will the neighbors think?* The same neighbors who had stood by impotent and now couldn't wait to get out of the church, to get away from the lifeless young woman whose death so shamed them, to get away from their annoyance and their utter guilt.

She couldn't breathe.

Wergild

She couldn't, she couldn't … she couldn't. By a power not her own, she found herself rising and walking the few paces to her sister's remains. She couldn't breathe, her throat so choked and frozen with emotion that not a word could come out. But when she went to speak, words burst from her like a thunderclap.

"Damn you all straight to Hell!!!" shouted a quavering voice she scarcely recognized. "You miserable, spineless curs! You men who are less than women! Less than children! Cower in your homes! Tremble in fear! It's all you're fit for! They hunt us like animals, they use us for sport, and you … you do … *nothing!"*

Her father, mortified, stood and approached her. It was as nothing to her that a man she'd loved and feared her entire life now, in anger, sought to corral and silence her.

A madwoman possessed her.

"And now you pray to this useless god. Where is he?! He's supposed to walk among us. Where is he?! You worship at an altar led by a priest who sucks the tit of the men who murder us. False priest, false god, false men!! *Damn the cowards of Edwin Township straight to Hell!"*

An iron grip seized her right shoulder, and she lashed out with all her might. The shocked look on her father's face as he stepped away moved her not at all. It was too late.

"And damn you, you miserable man," she spat at him, her voice still choked with rage. "I'll have what's mine. I'll have my vengeance. *I'm going to the Fiend!"*

Deirdre fled through the church doors and made a hard right for the trail to the upper meadow. She'd never before been to the barrow, but everyone knew where it was. It was the place in the far distant woods to which no one ever ventured. None who still lived had ever seen the Fiend that lived there, but it was known without dispute that was its lair. Three wretched souls in Deirdre's fourteen years, fools all, had taken the journey, had travelled to Blackwood Barrow, a place only the most desperate or pathetic dared.

None had returned.

Three years before, the affianced of Deirdre's murdered brother, Beleric, had been the last. For three days, an armed group from the township had scoured the woods around the barrow looking for sweet Twila Gandy. The men hadn't the nerve to seek justice for Beleric, but they'd at least searched for the girl. It had been the last act of courage in Edwin Township.

Deirdre continued at a run as she passed the upper meadow. Her long and strong legs propelled her through the dense copses where the timbermen worked, past the wooded hummocks where the crofters foraged, and into the Blackwood where only the hunters dared go.

By that time, the thicket had slowed her to a walk, but her entire course had been beset by the water that streamed from her eyes and the heaving sobs that racked her grieving body. The past was gone, everything was dead and gone, and she could never return.

Many was the silent night she'd lain awake wondering what had become of Twila, whether the Fiend had dragged her to Hell, or bandits had made off with her. Only Fiona's warm and loving reassurances in the bed they'd shared had comforted her. Now, all gone.

So, she continued on her path, which by that time had narrowed to a faint trace leading ever northward into the hills.

It wasn't clear how much time had passed when she stumbled upon a faint clearing in the forest. Her stomach rumbled, and the sun seemed near its zenith, but she hadn't thought to bring anything to eat. She continued onward into the clearing that appeared to be some sort of footpath, one far wider than necessary for the passing of game.

It was only when she made the third turn along the winding way that she was accosted by a voice.

"May I help you?"

The deep and buttery voice had come so abruptly that she leapt in the air, and now a tense and trembling Deirdre peered into the shade of the nearby wood to determine its source. At first, there was nothing. And then she discerned — or she thought she discerned — a figure near the bole of a large maple at ten paces distant. She dared not go closer but instead sidestepped for a better angle and peered more closely.

"What brings you up into the Blackwood?" the voice intoned in the deepest bass. "I don't often get visitors out this way."

The new words sent another jolt through her, but soon after, her eyes focused, and she made out the shape of what could only be the ugliest and dirtiest little man she'd ever seen. He squatted on his heels just inside the shade of the maple and regarded her carefully.

She moved to speak, and nothing came out. Was this some vagrant? A highwayman in the hills who preyed on the lost and the desperate? The villain seemed filthy enough to do most anything, and his voice was … there was a cream, a honey, a smoothness to it that set her nerves on edge.

"I …," she finally managed to spit out. She otherwise stood trembling while twisting and wringing her fingers in front of her, as if that act might ward off some menace. "My … m …," she tried to continue, uncertain what to say, if anything. The man seemed small, and she was a swift runner. The mere thought of running caused her muscles to bunch for just that purpose.

But before she could think to bolt away, the man leaned forward and stood erect to his full height. In two strides, he stood in the path before her, and he was simply gigantic, at least half again as tall as the tallest man in the township and equally lean and powerful. What had seemed dirt and soil upon his flesh now appeared to have been an illusion, as thorough as his sudden change in size, for his skin was mottled and dark, colored in shades of black, grey, and sickly blue. His eyes … his eyes were jaundiced orbs, and there was no hiding his teeth. Even with a mouth half-closed, the tips of grisly canines were visible top and bottom.

Deirdre's sturdy farm legs betrayed her, and she soon found herself supine on the ground, where a horrid smell assaulted her.

She'd soiled herself.

The Foreigner

Isabel stared down shocked and terrified at the broken and lifeless body before her, the body of a man who had been her friend and protector, and to her horror and shame she found herself only able to tremble at her own future.

She'd never seen a dead body before arriving in the kingdom of Albion a year before, but she'd seen many since. This was a violent land of warlike folk, and Isabel Castellan, late of Savannah, Georgia, was a radio DJ who had a Friday-night talk show to which no one ever listened. One year before, she'd wanted nothing more than to take a long weekend of hiking and camping at Blood Mountain to clear her head and to chart her future. Instead, her future was decided for her. After three days lost in the woods, she'd emerged at a small hamlet in the County of Blenheim, in a place called Albion, and she had no idea how to find her way back home.

Sir Utrecht Simon had been her savior, the true knight in shining armor she had never believed actually existed. Well, his long chainmail armor hadn't shone quite so bright, but he was kind, brave, and patient. And he had taken her in after the wretched farmer, who first had sheltered her, had demanded certain compensations for his troubles.

The young knight had demanded no such intimacies, but had befriended her and given generously of his guidance and protection. She had abided with him for nearly a year at a small blockhouse in northern Blenheim, where she'd learned the local dialect, which was surprisingly similar to English once she'd worked out the complex flow of it, and had come to understand the local customs.

She and Sir Utrecht had traveled and visited with neighbors and friends often. Two days before, they'd arrived at the manor house of a local aristocrat, Sir Reynard Lisle, a friend of the Simon family. The assembly had been large and diverse, but the looks she'd received from some of the knights and nobles at the small festival should have told her to run. But Sir Utrecht was there, and he'd assured her there was nothing to fear.

Late the evening before, a quarrel had erupted between Sir Utrecht and a nobleman, Sir Etienne de Margot, by all accounts a man of wealth and influence. Such things weren't uncommon among an armed and honor-bound gentry. Yet Isabel's senses had told her something was not right this time. Utrecht was brave and strong, but in her time with him, she'd not known him to seek a quarrel with anyone. And his reassurances prior to the duel had not comforted her.

And now her friend and protector lay dead, and something still was terribly wrong. None of his friends or retainers had hastened to his assistance when he fell — clearly his wound was mortal, his death quick — but neither had any ventured to recover his body. Even now, she felt the mood had shifted ever so subtly. No one present had moved to comfort her in the way she'd come to recognize as typical after a single combat. There was something wrong, something terribly, terribly wrong.

Above the shouts and cheers of the entourage of de Margot, the pompous tenor of the nobleman himself could be heard. He praised the now-dead Utrecht for his courage and honor — such things were the custom in this strange and demented land — but even as she listened, still gripped by shock and fear, she discerned from his thick and cultured Ghitland accent a declaration that, naturally, he would undertake the protection of Lady Isabel.

Those last words should have come as a surprise to her, but they did not. She'd never been vain, never thought of herself as a great beauty, but everything she'd sensed the last two days had told her that an all too typical and pathetic male lust and covetousness was the cause of the tension around her. Etienne de Margot wanted her, and he was willing to kill a noble young knight to have her.

Her passage back to the tent was easy. No one wanted to see her. Strangers didn't know her, and those with whom she was familiar didn't now have the heart to meet her eyes. Back at the pavilion, she grabbed her rucksack and shoved her meager belongings within. She was mere feet outside the tent and moving toward a nearby tree line when strong hands accosted her, rushing her along and whispering in her ear.

"Go west, follow the main road, but don't stay *on* the road. They'll be looking for you." These were the words of Lewis Ville, a friend of Utrecht and the master of hounds for Sir Reynard Lisle. She and the huntsman reached the woods, and he hurried her along. "Sir Etienne means to have you for his cousin Sir Everett Dupuis."

"Why ...?" she finally began.

"Lady Isabel, I know your ways are different, and I wouldn't wish Dupuis on any woman ... neither would Utrecht." He stopped and pointed. "Go that way, follow the setting sun, and keep the King Star on your right at night. I'll run the hounds in a different direction, but that will only delay them so long. Stay out of sight and keep heading west, and in a week or ten days you'll come to the lands of Sir Brian Mayfield, a friend of Sir Utrecht. Tell him your tale; he will shelter you."

Isabel hesitated, wanting to thank the man, to throw her arms around him — but yet uncertain how she would make such a journey alone in a violent land.

"Child, hurry," was his urgent plea.

With a nervous nod, she thanked him and fled into the forest.

Blackwood Barrow

The Fiend — for this creature clearly was it — stared down to where Deirdre lay on the ground. After some moments, the monster spoke with a slight gesture.

"There's a stream yonder, 'round the next bend, if you want to clean yourself." The enormous thing strode in the direction indicated without further word.

Deirdre wanted nothing more than to fly, to flee, to jump up and get away. But in the end, her pain and rage were greater than her terror. She would stay, because she had to. The screaming in her head would brook no other action. She would stay and sell her soul.

And yet, it took her some minutes to quell the trembling in her body and to rise from the ground.

By that time, the Fiend had passed around the bend in the path to which he'd recently pointed. His absence made rising possible, but when she came awkwardly to her feet, Deirdre stood for some minutes, head down, moving her feet in place as if that mere action would propel her toward her destination. She was frightened beyond words, but slowly, ever so slowly, in mincing steps, she began to creep after the Fiend.

It was a walk that should have taken mere moments, but it must have taken nearly an eighth of a bell. And when next she spied the Fiend, it was sitting on a broad patch of grass beside a quiet stream, its legs spread before it, elbows on knees, gazing into the forest beyond. Nearby, there was a broad pool formed on a bend in the stream, and it was to that spot Deirdre slowly repaired. The Fiend appeared to pay her no mind, and she struggled not to look in its direction.

Thankfully, as she often did, she'd donned that morning knee britches under her dress and did not have to bear the shame of undressing completely before the monster. Still, it took her some time to wiggle from her britches, clean herself, and then properly launder her garments, both inners and outers. All the while, the Fiend sat patiently, apparently disregarding her entirely. Its mere presence caused her to shake uncontrollably and for her breath to come in shallow pants.

The young Surrey girl had never been so frightened.

But her inner torment would not allow her to leave, and the moment she finished her ablutions and rearranged her now damp dress, she walked, head down and in short steps, toward the lawn where the Fiend was couched. Stopping ten paces before it, she struggled to speak.

"You should run along home, now," it said. "Your parents will be missing you." Its voice was still deep and malevolent, but it lacked the buttery cream of before.

It took Deirdre some moments to compose herself. "I can't go back."

"Nonsense," replied the Fiend. "Are your parents looking to marry you to some toothless imbecile? Is that it? You look to be of an age. I assure you, it won't be all that bad. Just run along."

True. Deirdre was fourteen, nearly of an age to marry, but ... "that's not it. I've come to sell my soul." Those last words left her as a mere squeak.

The Fiend sighed. "Oh ... that again. Not in the market."

An upset yelp of protest escaped her before she could think.

"Child," the Fiend continued, "you humans put far too much stock in the worth of your souls. I'm here to tell you, after long study and careful consideration, the human soul isn't worth a tuppence. Now, good day." Somehow the Fiend rolled to its feet, again towering over Deirdre, before turning and again striding away.

That couldn't be it.

That couldn't be all.

This ridiculous journey was all she had, her only hope, her only chance at justice, at vengeance. The injustice of the whole embarrassing episode fueled her anger and remorse and, with her still soggy britches in hand, she ran after the Fiend, whose long legs carried it at a great pace.

"I ... I ...," she voiced several times in succession as she jogged to keep up, before finally shouting out, "I can't go back. I can't. *I can't*." Her final words were nearly a scream.

The Fiend, who'd appeared not to regard her as he'd moved to depart, looked down now and then came to a halt. The creature gazed at her carefully, as if waiting for her to speak.

"I ...," she again sputtered. "There's nothing left. They took everything ... my brother, my sister. And no one will do anything ... *anything*. I need to do *something*!" A terrible trembling beset her, a worse quaking even than inspired by the Fiend. "I'm not going back," she blubbered. "I can't."

Wergild

The Fiend bent forward slowly, until its face scarcely was a hand's width from hers. "Child, it's a terrible, terrible world full of terrible, terrible people. People come here often seeking from me their fair quarter, their pound of flesh. And, true, I could kill a few people for you ... but other villains would come to take their place. Nothing would change. And you'd be right back where you started, except you'd still need to pay me my toll...."

"I'll pay anything," she snapped. "*Anything*."

What could only be a weary look passed across the Fiend's dark and grisly face. It stood again to its full height and seemed about to speak.

At that very moment, Deirdre's stomach gave a long and savage growl. A moment of silence followed before the Fiend spoke.

"No wise decision was ever made on an empty stomach. I have a cottage yonder. Come along, and I'll feed you." The Fiend continued to speak as it turned to go, saying, "It's just lettuce and twice-baked beans. I won't make you eat the hocks of a hellhound."

The youngster still needed to jog to keep up, but some minutes travel found them at what appeared to be a thatch cottage amid the forest. There was a small garden plot nearby, a coop with a number of chickens, and a wood rick and shed. The place appeared no different than that inhabited by any small farmer or woodland crofter.

The Fiend led her inside, bending over nearly double to fit through the door, and directed her to a table on the far side of the room. After hanging her britches to dry on a ledge, she obediently sat and waited while her host puttered about a small cooking area. It was only after some time that it appeared by some outlandish magic that the creature's dimensions again had changed. The Fiend now was of no greater height than a tall man. And its form wasn't quite so tattered. Its looked more the grimy and soiled article that she'd first spied in the woods.

After a short time more, the creature lay before her a plate of beans, bread, and greens, as well as some eating utensils, before taking a seat opposite. He — for the Fiend now appeared more a *he* than an *it* — sat patiently as she ate.

No time at all passed before Deirdre was finished, and when she sopped the last of the beans from the platter with the last of her bread, it occurred to her he'd eaten nothing. She looked up toward his human-like face without thinking.

"Thank you," she said out of habit.

The Fiend reached over and slid her platter aside. "What am I to do with you?"

"I want vengeance." This time her voice was somewhat meeker, but with the same resolve.

"Everyone does," he said with a sigh. "And who do you want this vengeance from?"

Tears again leapt to her eyes. "Those who defiled and murdered my sister ... and those who killed my brother."

"What are their names?"

"I ... I don't," she whispered. She continued more loudly. "But I know they're Gheets. It's been like that my entire life! They're...."

"I know about the war," he said patiently. "Your side lost. It's ever the way of things."

"But there was a treaty," she protested.

"Which favored the Gheet and the Surrey nobility and gentry. You Surrey free farmers — and I can tell from the look of you, your folks are free farmers — you all got the worst of it."

"Then you'll help?"

"Child, who am I to avenge you against? The entire Gheet race?"

Deirdre desperately wanted to say yes. But the truth was no one but the felons themselves knew who'd brutalized, raped, and murdered Fiona. The tearful young woman had a better idea of who struck down Beleric, but, even then, his attackers were many and the one who cast the murderous blow.... No one knew.

Her silence was her answer.

"I'll make you a deal, child," said the Fiend, breaking the silence. "But you have to swear to abide by it."

There was no hesitation in Deirdre's vigorous nod. "I swear it."

"My first condition is that you don't be hasty in striking a bargain," he continued. "Whatever offer I make you, you will agree to stay here and work as my servant for a month before giving me an answer. Is it agreed?"

"Yes." She again nodded.

"Very well. I offer you this. At the end of one month, if you still are so keen on the letting of blood, I will snatch seven souls for you. Seven murders I will do. In exchange for that tiny consideration, you will work as my servant for the rest of your life." He gave a negligent waggle of the fingers of one hand. "You can keep the soul."

Wergild

The young woman took in a breath to speak, but the Fiend raised a finger.

"Stay here for now," he admonished. "In one month, we will speak again. You do agree to that tiny precondition?"

Deirdre again nodded vigorously. "I do, but…."

"Just cooking and cleaning, child, and a bit of tending the garden. I'll not ask you to dispose of corpses or oversee demonic rites."

She wanted to ask whether keeping house would be her duties for the first month only, but thought the better of it. Though her pain had not eased, this small step toward retribution did ease her worry about the future. One way or the other, she would have her revenge. No matter what.

It occurred to her that the Fiend was regarding her with care.

"Get that silly grin off your face, child. You'll find a cot in the other room. Go to sleep. I'll fetch you when I need anything."

The young woman didn't hesitate but bounded to her feet and stepped lightly into a small chamber beyond. The room was tidy, and the bed was soft, but all she could think of was her vengeance.

The Flight

Isabel followed a course westward that paralleled the road, but at a distance. So carefully and cautiously had she moved over the past four days that it was unlikely anyone had seen her. The young woman was no great artisan of backwoods living, but she'd always enjoyed hiking and camping, and a year in Albion had taught her caution. A breakneck race through the forest not only would have exhausted her, but it would have betrayed her presence to those who searched for her and to any others who might mean to do her harm. There were bandits about, and Albion was a land in which many men considered a woman found alone to be a piece of fruit free for the picking.

So, she moved slowly and quietly.

There hadn't been time to prepare, but she'd had the presence of mind to toss some bread, cheese, and sausage into her rucksack, and she had her trusty hiking boots. After the first day's journey, she'd even resolved to slip on her cargo pants and sweatshirt. The plain woolen dress — one of many simple, but generous, gifts from her friend Utrecht — went into the ruck. No one would mistake her for a man, at least not close up, but unencumbered she could run if she must, and her tall and lean body always had been swift.

The food she'd grabbed gave out on the morning of the third day, but she wasn't too worried. The farm wives and crofters in the area around Utrecht's stronghold had taught her something of what was and was not safe to eat thereabouts, but she couldn't subsist long on roots and berries alone — already her stomach had begun to register complaints. And she wasn't perfectly certain how to find this Sir Brian, or even if she'd gotten his name right. Utrecht had never mentioned the man, but the young knight had spoken well of Lewis and had considered the master-of-hounds a friend. Isabel had little choice but to trust the man's guidance and to pray that Sir Brian was the type of person the huntsman claimed.

It was now midday on her fourth day of travel, and from the comings and goings she'd seen from afar, she suspected she was approaching a populated area. At least thirty miles now lay between her and pursuit —

or so she hoped — but strangers in a land such as this were presumed to be enemies. If she was spotted, even at a distance, there was no guarantee word of it wouldn't make its way back to de Margot and his followers.

And, yet, she had a bit of silver tucked away. A town meant an inn, and an inn meant food and almost certainly information. The accent with which she spoke the local dialect had raised no eyebrows. It might be worth the risk to venture among folk. There had been no sign of armored or mounted searchers. What's more, if she were to be espied by a local, might it not be better if she were seen walking down the main road in her dress rather than skulking about in the bushes dressed as a refugee from a Columbia Sportswear ad?

A little more information was in order, so she continued westward, skirting what looked to be several small cottages and dashing silently across a number of sideroads. Unquestionably, there were more people about, and, by early afternoon, the woodlands gave way to a broad open field that was transected by what looked to be several main roads or highways (or what passed for such things in Albion) that met near a large inn. There were a good many people about — twenty or thirty, at least — and it might be a good opportunity simply to make like another traveler and blend in.

Once she made her decision, she didn't tarry. Doffing her hiking attire, Isabel swiftly wiggled back into her woolen dress and sandals. After stashing her ruck under a pile of leaves, she took a long look around and made her way to the road. Her first steps on the packed-earth thoroughfare left her breathless and trembling, but she calmed herself and took up what she hoped was a natural gait. Within ten minutes, a shortcut took her into the pasture that fronted the inn, whose sign identified it as the Four Quarters.

The sound of children laughing drew her eye to a man of mature years leading a large horse in a circle by a long tether. Atop the powerful beast, a half dozen scruffy young urchins were squealing and laughing and clinging onto the plodding mount as if for dear life. As she passed, she next noticed a sullen young woman seated on the ground near a saddle. The lass's ocean of dark red hair and broad and flat nose marked her as a Surrey peasant or farm girl. Closer to the gates of the inn, five or so others lounged in the grass in various places, as if recovering from a long and wearisome journey.

The whole scene was idyllic, simply pristine in that way picture postcards sometimes were — until the sound of approaching horses caught her ear. From the corner of her eye, Isabel saw five mounted knights approach the inn at a gallop. Among them was Sir Etienne de Margot.

The Knight

Time flowed differently in the Fiend's tiny slice of the world — or so he claimed — and it had left Deirdre with deeply mixed feelings to find that her brother's betrothed, sweet Twila Gandy, had indeed found the Fiend three years ago, but that somehow the monster had tempted her to forswear her rage and to remain in the peace and tranquility of his hidden world, a place in which Twila had lived a long and contented life, before succumbing to old age some time before.

It seemed an absurd tale, and Deirdre only had the grave marker the Fiend had shown her as tangible proof of it. But the sadness in his eyes upon the showing of it convinced her the Fiend's words were true.

Deirdre believed him when he extended her the same offer, but she refused to be swayed. There was no "peace" in her now. No, a month had passed, and time had not slackened Deirdre's unquenchable thirst for retribution.

The screaming in her mind, the hungering in her heart, and the insatiable need for vengeance would not die, and it would not be quelled, or bribed, or reasoned with. On the thirtieth day of her first arriving in the barrow, she told the Fiend she was ready to go. She wanted her seven murders, and she would settle for not one soul less.

The Fiend merely sighed. And the two departed without further word and with no additional preparations. The Fiend assured her that they had all they would need, for all they needed was within her. It wasn't clear what such a thing meant, but she didn't quarrel.

They made first for Portsmouth, a harbor town near the eastern sea. She could make nothing at all of what the Fiend intended, and with a stoic silence, he resisted all of her attempts to direct or instruct him. He merely noted that there was something at Portsmouth he needed to find, some tiny slice of information that "the wind" would not or could not tell him. He often talked in such peculiar ways, and over the past thirty days, he'd spent much of his time sitting on a large stone near the barrow simply ... sitting. He claimed he was listening to the wind. Deirdre didn't know.

"Tuppence," he said after they'd been on the road to Portsmouth for a time — he'd immediately taken to calling her that after her decision to stay at the barrow — "if you're willing to listen and know how, the wind will tell you most of what you need to know."

"For instance?"

"For instance," he began, "there is a story to be had there."

"A story?"

"Yes, a good and honest story. You like stories, don't you?"

Indeed, Deirdre did like stories, and the Fiend had regaled her with a long litany of them during their month at the barrow. (It shamed the grief-stricken lass deeply that she'd enjoyed each and every one, so she refused to share that particular fact with her companion.) "I do like stories," was all she was willing to admit. "What's this one about?"

"It's about a good and noble knight who has come home from a long journey only to find sadness."

"How is that a good story?" she asked, perhaps a bit peevishly.

"Because, Tuppence, you and I are going to write that story a happy ending."

The Fiend said no more on the matter, but over the next few hours as they walked and chatted, making their way east from the barrow, through the forest, and down to the piedmont, another of his many and subtle changes unfolded.

Quite without her noticing, the Fiend slowly had transformed from the scruffy old ragamuffin with whom she was familiar to a good and proper man, all during the course of the morning. By the time they reached a small inn that the Fiend said was the halfway point to Portsmouth, he was a downright normal fellow, indistinguishable from any other, save, perhaps, he was taller and much stronger looking than most. With his tawny hair and gray eyes, he might have passed for a man of the northern Surrey.

She hadn't realized fiends could do such things, but neither did she know much of barrow fiends and their fiendish ways, only what she'd heard in the village and at school. It was likely not everything made it into books, she supposed.

After their lunch at the inn, of which the Fiend scarcely participated, the transformation continued, again without Deirdre at first having noticed. During the afternoon, it became apparent that the Fiend sported a new attire. First, it was leather breaches and a short but sturdy leather vest, and then, again with Deirdre having not seen the transformation, he walked beside her in a long chainmail hauberk. Next came a metal half-helm on a tether at his waist, a long narrow shield across his back, and a sword in a scabbard at his side. No sooner had this last accoutrement appeared than they reached a stable, where the Fiend acquired two mounts, a healthy courser for him and a gentle palfrey for her.

To her eternal shock, Deirdre realized the Fiend had transformed himself over the course of the day into a mounted Gheet knight.

"Have you never ridden a horse?" he asked in response to the long and horrified look she gave him.

"It's not that." She actually *never had* ridden a horse. "But…."

"It's still me under here," he whispered in a voice the stable's groomsman couldn't overhear. The smile he flashed said he knew he needn't bother being secretive. "Just call me Sir Alexis if anyone asks. You're my ward."

Deirdre nodded before giving a dull reply. "I'm your ward."

"Yes, my ward, Tuppence. I took you in when you were but a sprout."

She nodded, again feeling at a loss.

"Good," he said patiently. "Now, stand to the left of the horse, place your left hand there on the pommel, and put your left foot in that notch."

With the Fiend's tutoring, she took to riding better than she ever would have imagined. It helped that the palfrey on which she rode was an unusually amiable animal, and during the remains of the day, they spent most of their time working on her riding skills as they travelled. She had to be an admirable rider, according to the Fiend — according to Sir Alexis that is — because their story had to be solid, consistent, and believable.

Once they reached Portsmouth, they took a room at an inn just outside the city gates, where the Fiend spent his days sitting, drinking, and laughing with passing Gheet gentry. During the in-betweens, the Fiend purchased for her various odds and ends, including several changes of clothes, each simple but finer than she'd ever known. She never thought to ask from whence came the money, but she did wordlessly ponder what method of repayment he might expect.

Finally, at the end of the second day, Deirdre had had enough. She hadn't been sleeping well — had not been since her bereavement — and her irritability had grown too much.

"Why are we sitting about doing nothing?" she growled as the Fiend tipped his third tankard of the morning.

"The wind can't tell me everything," was his patient reply. "I need to know many things if I am to be a proper Gheet knight."

"And why wou…," she began.

"Can you think of a safer way to travel in County Blenheim, child?"

She blushed all of a sudden. He had a point.

"For what I am to do, Tuppence, I need to know things … and to draw close to people. Can you trust me?"

"I can," she said with a nod. "But … but, what … why do you need to draw close…?"

"Child, can you imagine that not every Gheet is a monster? And that there might be some few good folk among them? People who might be useful tools and helpers in our endeavor?"

Deirdre was at a loss. Her entire being had so raged this last month with anger, outrage, and a thirst for reprisal that she could neither think nor see in any colors but those. True, in the past there had been Gheet within their community who weren't terrible folk, but those were the same Gheet who would commiserate with Surrey farmers during their mourning and then later lounge laughing with the worst of their Gheet tormentors at an inn or tavern. They all deserved the gibbet, all of them … and worse.

"Tuppence, I don't have a plan, not a proper one," he said in a soothing way. "So, I need to learn. And trust me when I say, not all Gheet are monsters."

"There sure are enough of them," she nearly shouted. "Bloodthirsty vermin."

"Aye," he agreed with a faint smile. "Some of them are killers, and killers of the worst kind. But there's a funny thing about those that love killing too much. They often are the very same folks who have a hard time telling friend from foe." He patted her shoulder gently. "Relax and enjoy the next few days. The weather is sunny and wonderful and the breeze fine. Would you like me to have the landlady bring some more berries for your cream?"

"Yes, please," she nodded. "And some more bread and some of the soft white cheese?"

Sir Alexis rolled to his feet to oblige her.

For the first time, Deirdre marveled at how patient he was with her. It simply wasn't something that had dawned on her before that moment. The truth was, she'd been so busy being furious and vengeful (both of which were now fulltime preoccupations) that his deportment hadn't occurred to her.

If anything, she may have pondered how he was a bit *too* amiable to be a Fiend, and several times the thought had flitted through her mind that perhaps the Fiend might not have the gusto to wreak havoc in a proper way, at least not in the way Deirdre felt it needed to be wreaked. He seemed overall too convivial. For all his alleged planning, he so far had named no victims nor given any inkling about what they might be about in their "endeavor," as he called it.

Well, she didn't know any other fiends, so she had to go with the fiend she had. Still, it wouldn't hurt to come up with a few plans of her own on how best to motivate the creature when the time came, to put a little pep in his step. Such a thing wasn't an easy task — this was all virgin territory for a Surrey farmgirl — but she'd work something out.

The next morning, the two departed Portsmouth and headed inland toward the town of New Market. Sir Alexis again was cagey about what they might find there, and Deirdre finally accepted the fact that the Fiend simply didn't have a clear sense of what they would do. They spent most of the day chatting, him telling her how to be a proper Gheet lady and her telling him to get bent. All the while, Deirdre pondered and stewed about how best to get the Fiend into full gallop — as he referred to a horse's fastest pace.

At some point in the afternoon, they came to a large intersection, and Sir Alexis announced the place would be an auspicious location to stop. (He said only that the wind augured well for it when she asked how he knew.) The place, which went by the name Inn of the Four Quarters, was pleasant and bustling. After taking a room and eating, Deirdre and Sir Alexis went to a pasture to join other travelers in resting and enjoying the day.

Deirdre wanted to have none of it and sat in sullen silence seething at yet another waste of time. While Sir Alexis, of all things, idled away the day playing with the local children and allowing them to pile on his courser, she sat with her back against the mount's saddle, sulking and trying her level best not to enjoy anything of the marvelous day with which they'd been blessed.

At a bell past midday, things went from bad to worse. About that time, a tall and regal woman with the telltale dark hair and olive complexion of a purebred Gheet emerged from the brush and made her haughty way toward the inn. It might have piqued Deirdre's interest that the woman had arrived afoot, but before she could think of it, the woman was standing beside her, looking down with the most desperate eyes.

She spoke in a strange accent, one that might have marked her as neither Gheet nor Surrey. "Please help me," she said in a voice that trembled. "Those men aim to harm me. I'm alone and afraid."

The woman began to cry.

The Foundling

In ordinary times, nothing would have frightened Isabel more than turning to complete strangers for help, but these were no ordinary times. The terror she felt at knowing that her life was not her own and that she no longer was the strong and independent woman she was in her life in Savannah left her numb and humiliated.

This indeed was a strange and mercurial land, and she could not stand alone in it. Without friends and without supporters, her hopes of keeping her freedom and her life were scanty or none. And even that security was illusory in ways she never could have imagined in her past life. The alacrity with which Utrecht's friends, all save one, literally had turned and walked away left her stunned.

And now de Margot was mere yards away, and she was standing friendless in an open field near the Four Quarters Inn. She'd never been so scared in her life.

"Please help me," she again implored in the local tongue. The sullen young woman with the luscious red hair looked up at her with what may have been surprise. It should have been no wonder. The Gheet long had treated the young woman's people with wanton brutality, and Isabel had the raiment, hair, and complexion of one of her oppressors.

"Are you in need of assistance, m'lady?" It was the voice of a man, the very same who moments before she'd seen making merry with a group of local children. He led his horse, now sans children, to where Isabel stood near the woman, regarding her carefully all the while.

Isabel turned to speak, and nothing came out. The man's appearance was that of one of the northern Surrey, with tawny hair and close-cut blonde whiskers, an appearance that had become common among the Gheet as they and the Surrey had intermarried in northern Albion. Though he spoke with a dialect common between Gheet and Surrey, it was clear to Isabel that this was yet another Gheet knight. She at once suspected speaking had been a mistake.

Before she could run, he spoke again.

"I'm Alexis de Vere," he said before gesturing to the ruddy lass. "And this is my ward, Tuppence." By that time, he'd come within arm's reach, and his voice had disarmed her. "Are you well? Is there something we can do?"

"I ...," she began with a swift glance toward the gate where the five knights, boisterous and loud, were dismounting. "That man there means me harm."

The knight with whom she spoke regarded the men but briefly. "And who are these knights?"

"I don't know them all, but the one with the short hair is Sir Etienne de Margot. He murdered a friend of mine and now means to make off with me." For just the briefest of moments, Isabel saw what she thought was a smile light the face of Alexis de Vere, but the look was gone so quickly that she wasn't sure she'd seen it at all.

The knight nodded. "He's a well-known and powerful baron, this de Margot." There came a gentle smile then twisted lips, and he gestured to the blanket spread before his saddle. "I forget myself, m'lady. Our table and board are meagre, but sit and refresh yourself. I'll allow no harm to come to a guest."

It occurred to Isabel as she sat and took an offered slice of bread that though often short on mercy, the Gheet were obsessive about form and manners. Hospitality was the cornerstone of their ethos. Though but a blanket in a field, where they now sat was Sir Alexis's home, and he would defend it against all comers. What might happen an hour hence she did not know, but for the moment she was safe.

Still, she made a point of sitting in such a way as not to be obvious to de Margot and his companions, who stood laughing and joking with several other newly arrived knights not fifty yards distant.

It was only after several minutes of polite but nervous conversation with Sir Alexis and his ward, who'd by then gifted Isabel with several grudging smiles, that she felt safe enough to explain her circumstances. She made only short reference to her origins — how to explain that? — saying just that she was from Evaria, a land across the sea to the south. She told them of her being stranded, of her rescue by Sir Utrecht, and of the murder of her protector. Those last words were the hardest.

Sir Alexis nodded comfortingly throughout. "It's the way of things in Albion, Lady Isabel. When a man is challenged, honor demands he accept.

Wergild

Although it does escape me why a fight to the death was necessary, both men were equally armed and armored. It's tragic, but it's our way."

"Was...." She hesitated, knowing the answer to the question, but a flicker of weakness and uncertainty hit her. "Was I wrong to flee?"

A look she couldn't decipher crossed the face of the knight. "I don't know this Baron de Margot, not personally. But I knew a cousin of his in the Holy Land, the same Everett Dupuis of whom you speak ... or at least I believe so. It's a common name. I never saw Dupuis as a kind or goodly man, but both he and de Margot are men of wealth and influence and would provide well for any lady they chose to take as ward." He raised his hand and gestured to the blanket on which they reclined. "Certainly, they could provide better than the castle made of wool Tuppence and I have to offer."

Isabel shook her head. "The man frightens me. I don't think he intends me well."

There again crossed the knight's face an inscrutable look. "Well, I don't know Brian Mayfield, but I'm acquainted with the reputation of the family. They are a fine and generous folk. And if I'm not mistaken, their estates lie three days journey past New Market. But ... Lady Isabel, Tuppence and I are on an errand that entails some danger...."

"Sir Alexis, I've come four days alone. I can travel another four." In truth, she was torn. The idea of trusting this kind and fearsome knight was seductive, but something told her she needed to proceed by herself.

"M'lady, it speaks well of you and your valor that you've travelled this far, but even in the best of times a young woman is not safe to travel unaccompanied." Again, there was that look on his face. "I don't mean to gainsay your feelings, but allow me to speak with Baron de Margot on your behalf. It may well be that his concern for you is sincere and he would be willing to see you safe to Mayfield."

"Sir Alexis ... I can't. There's no way for me to explain, but a woman knows." Isabel glanced to Tuppence, who gave Sir Alexis a knowing nod and a shrug.

The knight for a moment was lost in thought, and Tuppence maintained her dour silence. He spoke at last. "If you intend to travel on alone, I'll ensure that de Margot and his men don't search for you further ... at least not today. Travel as you did before, away from roads and people, and when you come to New Market, find a man of god named Ainsley. I knew him as a pilgrim in the Holy Land. He will help you."

For a moment she was overwhelmed. The knight and his ward had done little, but that mere dram of kindness had filled her with hope. "Thank you."

The knight stood and began to prepare his chainmail, which he'd recovered from the ground near the saddle. "No need to thank for a duty, Lady Isabel. Stay here for a time with Tuppence. She'll give you provisions for your trip. I go to introduce myself to de Margot and his lot." He gave her a wink. "Perhaps I'll show the baron to the tilting yard for a few lessons."

She felt the breath suddenly leave her and opened her mouth to protest.

"Calm yourself, m'lady," he said with a smile. "Like as not, we'll retire to the alehouse. The moment we're out of sight, you take your leave. Tuppence will give you anything you need."

With that, the great knight turned and strode to the gate of the inn. Within moments, voices were raised, and it seemed there might be violence — she couldn't bring herself to look in that direction — but soon after, the bullying tones were replaced with barks of laughter and, so it seemed, Sir Alexis repaired himself to the alehouse, de Margot and his knights in tow.

When Isabel rose onto shaky legs moments later, Tuppence already had a bag prepared for her. The dour young woman seemed as if she might speak and after a brief hesitation turned to a bag near the saddle and recovered a long dagger in its sheath. This she handed to Isabel. There was a look of compassion on the young woman's face that had not been there before.

"Good luck, Lady Isabel, and be careful." They were the first proper words Tuppence had spoken since Isabel had arrived.

After a short and impulsive hug, Isabel turned and fled the way she'd come.

The Barrow Boy

Deirdre wasn't angry with Sir Alexis. His sympathy for beautiful young Lady Isabel earlier in the afternoon was understandable — the woman truly seemed in desperate need of succor, even if she was a Gheet — but to Deirdre, it was yet another sign of the Fiend's sappy and tender underbelly. If this was what passed for a fiend, Deirdre should have saved herself the trouble and sought the assistance of a barnyard kitten.

The "ferocious and diabolical" Sir Alexis, as Deirdre sullenly came to think of him, spent the balance of the afternoon and much of the evening hoisting wine, beer, and ale with Etienne de Margot and a handful of the baron's knights. As Alexis had promised, he kept the crowd busy, so busy that the warriors forsook for a time their search for the "spritely hart" and indulged themselves with their new boon companion.

Deirdre was dejected. Sitting alone at a table in the corner, she passed the evening nibbling away in an orgy of gustatory extravagance that at any other time in her life would have left her delirious. Time and again, it came to her how Fiona would have reveled in such an evening, a memory of her sister so painful and bitter that it stole away even Deirdre's tears.

Of course, de Margot was every inch the vicious swine Isabel had described — what else would a Gheet baron be? A half dozen times throughout the evening, the baron had leapt to his feet at some imagined slight from Sir Alexis, whose only reaction to de Margot's threats of violence was to throw up his hands and speak words of appeasement and peace. On those occasions, the only thing that stopped de Margot from giving Alexis a good and hard clout was the timely intervention of one of de Margot's companions, a hirsute and bulky knight she'd several times heard called de Bois-Guilbert.

She'd ignored the occasional taunt from the men that spoke of Alexis's 'Surrey wench,' but instead sipped mulled wine and nibbled tarts and cherry jelly. The food was delightful, but it was getting her no closer to justice. She wanted to hate Sir Alexis ... she wanted to hate the Fiend. He was just too amiable. So, she abided the evening, alternating between fury and sulkiness and eventually falling asleep with her head on the table she occupied in the corner.

Deirdre awoke from a troubled slumber the next morning in the softest bed in which she'd ever lay. The Devil only knew how she got there. Her clothes were still on, and the small satchel with her belongings was placed carefully on a table near the door. From the look of the sky, it was just before dawn, and neither the Fiend nor any of his effects were to be seen. Likely he awaited her at the stable. (She remembered him saying something about an early start, but there was still a bit of wine in her head.)

Making a quick toilet, she checked to see if she had all her belongings and headed toward the stable. Several of the baron's men were passed out in the great room's various nooks and crannies, though there was no sign of the nobleman himself — just as well that. In the stable, she found the blacksmith and his assistant stoking the day's fire. The only other person present was a lone barrow boy of about ten years with a barrowful of produce, who looked to be beginning his day.

Before she could round the building and look in the pasture, the lad spoke up.

"Come along, Tuppence. We've an appointment to make on the road to New Market. It's miles to go before we rest. I have your breakfast here, so we can eat on the road."

She stared at the lad, a fresh-faced youth and one of the prettiest creatures she'd ever seen. She moved to open her mouth.

"Tuppence," said the boy with a sweet smile and a hint of mock exasperation, "I thought the barrow would be a dead giveaway."

Wergild

Part II
The Seven

"Ye may read all the learn'd treatises, tracts, and monographs ye want, but t'end of the day, e'ry right-minded soul, thru 'is own wit and commonsense, knows there's things from which ye' need refrain. Stay the Hell away from sin!
... unless ye must."

—***The Venerable Wooster, Vicar of Curmudge***

Wergild

Lust

"From a purely academic standpoint, I've always favored lust."
—**De Diabolicum,** *author unknown*

The barrow boy was a pretty and pleasant lad who appeared to be about three or four years Deirdre's junior, and over the course of the next few hours, she and the now pint-size Fiend ambled down the High Road to New Market, hawking his produce, chatting with passersby, and making their leisurely pace westward. At any other time, it would have been a delightful day, but as in the preceding days with Sir Alexis, they were getting nowhere. And it hadn't escaped Deirdre's notice that she was no longer in the company of an armed and armored Gheet knight. These were dangerous times, and they trod a path not too many miles distant from where monsters had stolen everything from her beloved sister.

As the morning passed, Deirdre, whose fury and anger were never far from the surface, felt burgeoning apprehension, which soon grew to nervousness, then moments of full-bloom fright. Every new traveler seen coming around a bend or over a rise stoked her apprehension. Yet the boy seemed unperturbed, though so different was he in appearance, deportment, and character from either the Fiend or Sir Alexis that, at first, Deirdre found it difficult treating the personable lad as the creature she knew him to be.

The guise the Fiend had assumed wasn't that of a typical farmhand by any means, but even that wasn't terribly surprising. Travelling vendors such as the one the Fiend now mimicked were not as common as they once had been (or so Deirdre had been led to believe), but they had a reputation of being tough, scrappy, and worldly, and even the lads among them had a ferocious repute.

But this lad? He was but a child, soft and innocent.

It was still some time before noon when she mustered the resolve to speak beyond their simple chit-chat.

"What became of Sir Alexis?" she ventured.

The lad gave her a beaming smile. "Oh, he'll be along. I'll keep you company until then, Tuppence." He hesitated before going on with a hint of apology in his voice. "I haven't put you off your game, have I? We've known each other over a month. I was certain you were accustomed to my ways."

The laugh Deirdre gave wasn't terribly convincing. "No. It's just a little surprising ... the suddenness of it. Why...?"

"I wanted to see the world through your eyes," the child-Fiend said with a laugh. He was several inches shorter than Deirdre and had a voice so sweet and high that it might have been that of a girl.

"It has to be more than that," she whispered. "What if we're set upon?"

"Tuppence!" the boy laughed even more loudly. "You forget who you're with. Besides, we won't meet anyone on this road who we don't want to meet."

"How do you know?"

Again, he flashed the boyish charm. "The wind told me."

By that time, a small knot of travelers had formed, and the boy deftly engaged in a series of trades and sales that netted them a small purse of copper. Despite several stops to eat and rest, their business was brisk for the rest of the day. And during that time, Deirdre, her apprehension of their predicament not totally forgotten, walked and seethed. This brisk exercise in free market trading didn't seem to be getting them anywhere, and she wanted her blood. She wanted blood, poison, fire, and vengeance. The screaming in her head wouldn't stop.

But throughout the day, the barrow boy just ambled toward New Market, the largest village in Deirdre's home township, selling this, that, and the other. He was friendly, kind, and patient to all comers, including Deirdre.

The makeup of passing travelers galled her even more. She'd seldom spent much time away from her home, but seeing now the way passersby came and went filled her with an additional fury. The few groups of Surrey farmers she saw (in a township that was mostly Surrey) went their way in groups of five or more, worried, probably concealing weapons, and intent on reaching their destination to the exclusion of all else. Many were the Gheet who travelled alone or in pairs, seemingly indifferent to their own safety. Some didn't even appear to carry weapons. The contrast between the groups they passed during the day was shocking and stoked her frightened and fuming heart.

As evening swiftly approached, they were still some miles from New Market, and the Fiend made no move to find them shelter. Deirdre's apprehension, which had ebbed and flowed throughout the day, bounded as she realized night soon would be upon them and the road suddenly was empty. The Fiend, though, continued to amble and to chatter in an affable fashion about the various amusing characters they had met during the day.

It was nigh on dusk when the final traveler of the day hove into view ahead, and it was some minutes more before Deirdre took full stock of the single mounted man. It was yet another several seconds for her to realize who he was. When she did, her blood froze.

The rider whose mount paced toward them was none other than Bertrand Servais, the chief magistrate of Blenheim County, a man whose disdain for the Surrey folk was well attested. None had ever known justice in his court, but instead were shown the door with a hard boot and warning about the penalties for perjury and for slandering honest Gheets.

As he approached them now, his fleshy and corpulent face was filled with hatred and rage.

———

"Boy," the county magistrate barked as he reined in his horse ten paces in front of them. "There are laws about street peddlers in this county. Come here!"

The boy went to lift his barrow.

"Leave it," the man commanded.

The boy did as he was told, stepped around the barrow, and in doing so flashed a smile to Deirdre that only she could see. The look on his pretty face sent her blood cold and set her to trembling. "I'll have his chitlins to sup," she thought she heard the Fiend-boy whisper in a voice like that of the Fiend she'd first met.

By that time, the magistrate had dismounted, and when the boy was before him, the man raised his riding crop and lifted the youngster's face with it. The man's voice was husky. "My, you are a pretty one."

It only was then Deirdre remembered the tales she'd heard of the magistrate, mere gossip she never had imagined true. Men didn't actually do such things to boys, did they?

Wergild

The magistrate said something else to the barrow boy, something so low that even at a scant ten paces Deirdre couldn't hear. The boy's quiet response apparently did not please the man, because he drew back the riding crop and struck the lad so hard across the face that it knocked him to the ground. By reflex, Deirdre stepped forward.

"Stay there, girl," the man barked. "I'll have my look at you next."

The barrow-boy was slow in rising. As he did, once again a look flashed across his face that only Deirdre could observe. Gone was the face, which moments before had been a canvas of such youthful beauty and innocence, supplanted by a malevolent and gleeful expression that caused Deirdre to let out a shriek.

"I'll have that thing you offered now, sir," said the boy in a meek voice before turning and springing at the magistrate.

Where once had been a boy's mouth, now there was an enormous gaping maw like that of a ravening predator, and that maw shot like an arrow for the tender spot of flesh beneath the magistrate's belt buckle, striking the portly man with such force that it lifted him from the ground. The Gheet worthy didn't even have time to shriek in pain or fear before the Fiend shook him hard three or four times like a dog thrashing about a rag toy. On the fourth such violent jolt, the magistrate flew from the grasp of the Fiend's ghastly fangs, sailing twenty or more paces down the road. The Fiend let out a hysterical cry into the heavens, and in one great bound flew to the back of the now rising magistrate and sunk his teeth into the nape of the gasping and whimpering man's neck.

As the Fiend's fangs found their mark, it was as if all the pigs in Albion had been cut at once. The noble Gheet screamed, screeched, squealed, and howled in terror and pain, and Deirdre, whose feet finally pulled free from where they'd been shackled to the ground, lost her balance, tripped over the barrow, and went tumbling head-over-heels down the steep bank beside the road. She landed in a great pile amid the thicket, and many moments passed before she untangled and righted herself.

By that time, the gleeful baritone howls of the Fiend rose in harmony with the terrified tenor screams and hysterical pleading of the wretched jurist.

Climbing hand over hand up the steep bank, Deirdre returned to the road just in time to see the magistrate, the Fiend now welded to the back of his neck in some farcical parody of a childhood piggy-back ride, running and jumping and staggering about, all the while twisting and shaking to remove the vicious parasite that gnawed upon his head. The blood flowed freely in great surges, and sufficient light remained for Deirdre to see the man was missing the skin from most of his face and the lower part of his right arm was hanging by a thread.

The Surrey lass was a farmgirl who'd many times slopped the abattoir, which was probably why she did not succumb immediately to nausea, but the tableau before her was so shocking and graphic that she crawled to the upturned barrow and, crouching behind it, hid her face in her hands and trembled at that ghastly symphony being played on the broad highway before her.

It was horrible, simply horrible, a condition she didn't think could grow worse until the shrieking was replaced by pathetic whimpering and the sounds of guttural and ravenous snarls, tearing flesh, and rapacious swallows. The poor girl gagged three times before crawling closer and pulling the upturned barrow atop her. She huddled beneath her makeshift tortoise shell for how long she did not know, covering her ears and trying not to cry.

The air in Deidre's makeshift shelter was just becoming unbearable when she heard a slight knock.

"Tuppence?"

"Are you going to eat me?" was all she could think to ask. Though weak, her voice didn't break when she spoke. For that paltry gift she was grateful.

"No," replied the barrow boy. "I couldn't eat another bite. But we have to get going."

The end of the barrow nearest her head rose a few feet from the ground. It was now full dark, but she could just make out the boy's angelic face.

"I'm sorry," he said. "I didn't mean to tease. But the night patrol will be out soon, and they'll arrive all the sooner if someone finds a riderless horse. We really need to go."

She hesitated, saying not a word.

"I really do promise," he said. "I would never eat you — you're not nearly old enough or fat enough for a proper meal. And I like you too much."

She hesitated, rising only when the boy lifted and righted the barrow onto the ground before her. She then rose and looked about as he collected their belongings and the few potatoes and turnips that remained from their cargo. It was too dark to see much, but there was a shoe lying on the ground in plain view some paces away. The thought that it might also contain a foot goaded her to action.

"Oh ... we really need to get going," she groaned. In an attempt to hold down her gorge, she covered her mouth and began jogging down the highway in the direction they had been traveling. The sound of the barrow rolling on the earth told her the boy was right behind her.

The boy soon caught up and after some time steered her to a low hill that was perhaps a furlong off the road. There, in some brush behind a copse of trees, the Fiend sat and urged her to rest. It took her only a short time to realize their location offered a clear view of the spot where the Fiend had gobbled up the magistrate — or the better part of him, as he several times corrected her — and left the man's remains along the highway. The Fiend meant to observe the effects of his handywork on the local constabulary.

Deirdre felt tired and faint but was unable to sleep a wink, troubled as she was by the ghastly memory of the Fiend's attack and by his long stream of hysterical giggles and near constant celebratory muttering. She only dozed once, and that was disrupted when the barrow boy woke her to leave. The night patrol had found the Fiend's dinner leftovers, and now he and Deirdre needed to quit the locality.

The boy led her across country in silence after that. She was grateful he returned to his earlier pleasant demeanor, but staying off the highway had slowed their pace, and it was hard going through the thicket. After several hours, the otherwise strong and fit girl very nearly collapsed, and before she could protest, the tiny barrow boy swept her up and placed her butt-first into the barrow, the manner by which she travelled for the last hour of their trip.

They only reached the inn on the outskirts of New Market as the sun threatened to illuminate yet another day, and Deirdre, still unable to sleep, was exhausted and feeling feverish when they did. It had been a frightening and troubling night. She didn't mean to be so cranky, but she started making outraged and fussy noises when the boy stopped the barrow and began speaking with someone she couldn't see.

They still hadn't reached the inn, and Deirdre lifted her head to look about and caught sight of the boy bent over and looking under some brush. Soon, another person came into view. It was the lovely Gheet woman they'd encountered two days before at the Four Quarters, Lady Isabel. Deirdre felt herself saying something, calling out to Isabel and the boy, but she didn't remember having formed the intent to speak. The effort of raising her head and making those utterances was more than Deirdre could bear, and when she leaned her head back onto the bag that was her pillow, she fainted away.

Gluttony

"Mind what you eat ... it could be the death of you."
—*Surrey Proverb*

The boy who woke her that morning was a complete stranger, but Isabel recognized the red-headed beauty who was with him. It wasn't readily clear why the young woman lay half-conscious in a wheelbarrow, but Isabel didn't see it as her place to ask. After a long day's walk and two frightening nights, one spent under the very bush from whence the boy had just roused her, she was grateful to see a familiar face, even that of the recumbent young woman.

"Are you a friend of Sir Alexis?" she asked the boy.

"Not exactly, miss. But I do run errands for him." The boy's accent was not cultured, but he was polite and seemed to be taking care of ... Tuppence. That was her name. "He said I was to keep an eye out for you, a foreign beauty with the eyes and coloration of a pureblood Gheet. You are Lady Isabel, then?"

"It was all just so sudden," Tuppence whimpered feebly from the wheelbarrow. "So ... sudden ... so ... terrib...."

Without thinking, Isabel crossed the ten feet to where Tuppence lay. She spoke to the boy. "I think she's delirious. Has she been hurt?"

"No, miss," said the sweet lad — he was such a lovely and well-mannered boy. "But we heard terrible sounds in the night, like some dreadful monster was stalking the land. It was all quite scary, and Tuppence took a fright. You're lucky you made it here from Four Quarters alone, miss."

Isabel nodded, more worried for the womanchild who lay before her. Tuppence was dour and laconic, but somehow, Isabel had taken an instant liking to her. "We should get her inside."

"You let me worry about that, Lady Isabel. You look just as tuckered." The lad took hold of the wheelbarrow and began moving the contraption toward the inn. "Hopefully they'll have some accommodation. I think

Miss Tuppence just needs a few hours rest and something to eat — as do you, miss."

Isabel secured her rucksack and followed immediately behind. It was only a few hundred paces to the inn, a place she had avoided the previous night for fear of being spotted by one of her pursuers, but the idea of staying in the forest yet another day frightened her more. The boy said there were monsters about, and she'd been in Albion long enough not to laugh at such words.

While Isabel watched over Tuppence, dampening her fevered brow with a wet cloth from the inn's fountain, the boy made his inquiries. The youngster was gone only a short time.

"The inn is full-up with Gheet worthies on their way to a tournament, miss. But I've spoken with the blacksmith. He has a room off the smithy where you and Miss Tuppence can rest for the day. That'll give us time to find other accommodations."

"Oh, please," she sighed, "lead the way."

The place the boy described was only a few dozen paces distant, and upon opening the door, Isabel was surprised. The room was small but remarkably tidy. There was a chair and but a single bed, one just wide enough for two small people. It was there the boy lay Tuppence.

As the youngster took off the girls boots and covered her with a blanket, Isabel marveled at the toughness of farm folk. The boy was slight, not over five feet, and couldn't have weighed more than ninety pounds. Yet he carried Tuppence with ease, and he fussed over her with a tenderness she wasn't accustomed to seeing in the male of the species.

"You should stretch out and get some rest too, Lady Isabel. Your bed for last night couldn't have provided much sleep."

"I'm fine, for now. Do you mind if I take the chair?"

The boy was sitting on the bed, still fussing over Tuppence, as a beloved brother might.

"Are you and Tuppence related?"

"Oh, no, miss," the boy smiled. "We of the barrow don't reckon kin in quite the same way as you'uns."

The barrow? She didn't understand. "How do you come to know one another?"

"Sir Alexis, miss. He set me to look over her and to find you. He's deeply sorry he couldn't have been here in person, but I'm to fetch

Wergild

Reverend Ainsley once I get you settled. The good reverend will do right by you."

An enormous weight was lifted from Isabel's spirit, and the possibility that there might be a light at the end of the tunnel — a light other than that of an oncoming train — filled her heart.

"If you don't mind me asking," the boy continued, "you're not from around these parts, are you, miss?"

The question took Isabel by surprise, not just because it seemed more insightful than she'd expected from a boy of no more than ten years. It was just…. She couldn't say but felt emboldened. "I grew up in a land far distant, one in which no one has ever heard of Albion or Ghitland or Evaria. It's another world altogether."

"You've come a far piece then, ain't you, ma'am?"

A tear leapt into her eye. "I have. And I worry I'll never find my way home."

"Many's the wicked folk in this world, ma'am, but many's the good. You'll find a place here, as I have."

The boy's words were another thing that didn't sound quite right, emanating as they did from the mouth of one so fresh, but Isabel was too exhausted to ponder anything further. She soon found herself nodding in the chair. After how long she knew not, a gentle shaking roused her.

"I'm off to find the reverend, miss. You best lock up after I go. These are rough and dangerous times. Oh … if I'm not here when he arrives, you'll know Reverend Ainsley. He's a great tall gopher with a gabby way about him."

She rose and by impulse gave the adorable lad a slight squeeze before letting him out and barring the door to their small lodging. The hammering of the blacksmith not twenty feet beyond the door bothered her not at all as she slipped into bed beside a fitful Tuppence and did her best to comfort the girl before herself falling off to sleep.

———

A still muddled Deirdre already was awake when she heard the knock at the door. She'd had the most dreadful nightmare — it was something about the magistrate — and she reached the door and was preparing to open it before she realized she didn't know where she was or how she'd gotten there. Her last memories were of the barrow and the boy and …

then she saw the sleeping beauty on the bed not five feet away. The woman was just opening her eyes.

There was another knock.

"Who is it?" she whispered at the wooden portal. The nearby banging of a hammer on anvil made it difficult to hear the answer, so she asked again, louder.

"Tuppence," said an unfamiliar voice that only could have belonged to one being, "it's your friend, Reverend Ainsley." Deirdre contemplated going back to bed, but sighed and opened the door to a tall man clad from head to toe in the humble black frockcoat and dark britches and stockings of an Unreformed preacher. Albeit strangely handsome, the Fiend in his new form was so lean and spare that missing a scant few meals likely would have rendered him cadaverous.

Of a sudden, Deirdre remembered the creature's last meal and felt a queasiness and slight tremor sweep over her. To her surprise, though, she felt no more fear for her companion's new incarnation than she had for his last. The memory of the evening before was ... well, it would take some getting used to, but the magistrate had been a scoundrel and a miserable pestilence on the land. Her dark fury, which was back with a vengeance, would allow that man no pity ... not much at least.

She realized the newcomer was addressing the woman on the bed.

"Lady Isabel," the man said, leaning toward her with the sweetest smile. "Allow me to introduce myself. I am the Right Reverend Moorcroft Ainsley, at your service." His slight forward lean turned into a somewhat inelegant bow. "Sir Alexis has relayed to me a missive on your troubles. And I do hope you will not hesitate to call on me for even the slightest service. I will endeavor mightily to see you done right by." He gently kissed her offered hand.

"Oh ... reverend. I'm overwhelmed. I ... I don't know what to say. Thank you."

Deirdre tried to keep from rolling her eyes. Instead she peeped out the door to where a hubbub alerted her to something outside the smithy that even the hammering of the anvil could not hide. "What's the commotion ... uh, reverend?" she asked the Fiend.

The reverend gave a pious sigh. "You ladies ought to stay inside for the nonce. It seems there's been a murder. The local magistrate was attacked by some sort of savage beast, and the locals and travelers both are in an uproar."

"Oh, my heavens," said Isabel. "The boy said something about a monster." She hesitated. "What was it?"

The Fiend-in-holy-orders struck a scholarly pose and after some scant moments spoke. "Had I access to my library, of course, I could consult the appropriate bestiary. But from the description given by those who stumbled upon the *locus in quo*, I'd have to presume the creature in question to be some sort of lycanthrope. Though ... it has been more than a century since such a being has been seen in these parts."

To Deirdre's eyes, it seemed Isabel was taken completely aback. "A werewolf?" the Gheet woman whispered in a husky voice.

The faux reverend replied with a solemn nod.

"Might it have been a fiend, instead?" asked Deirdre in all innocence.

Reverend Ainsley missed not a beat, but again took chin in hand. "It seems unlikely," he replied after a moment's learned contemplation. "The common fiend seldom ventures far from its barrow. Though I suppose it's a potentiality that can't be disregarded in its entirety."

For the first time, Deirdre realized the reverend spoke perfect Midland common with just a hint of a lisp, the kind of affectation the lesser Surrey gentry sported to sound more citified. The Fiend had pulled out all the stops in contriving its newest persona.

"Is it safe to travel?" Isabel asked. There was sincere worry in her voice. "Is it even safe to stay here?"

"Lady Isabel," the preacher responded with great reassurance, "such creatures do not make themselves known during the hours of daylight. But I would ask you to stay here with sweet Tuppence with the doors barred while I settle the crowd that has gathered without. In frightening times, the common folk need a steady shepherd to guide the way. I shall return in no time."

At about that moment, there was another knock on the door, and a man's heavy voice tinged with worry called out. "Reverend Ainsley, you're needed outside."

The beanpole smiled, bowed, and excused himself. Deirdre barred the door behind him, after which she sat on the bed next to Isabel. The Gheet woman bit at her thumb. The worry on her face was etched deep.

Deirdre was perplexed. How had Reverent Ainsley already made himself so known among the locals they would seek out his help? And then she remembered he was a fiend. There was no duplicity or subterfuge beyond him — or so she'd come to learn.

Her thoughts next flew to the ghastly vista from the night before. What had driven the Fiend to — she had to steady her stomach. What had prompted him so thoroughly to eviscerate the local magistrate? Did this count as one of her seven murders? Or was the scoundrel just freelancing? Doing a bit of moonlighting when he was supposed to be fetching up her vengeance? She found herself scowling and knitting her brow at the thought. Then again, maybe the Fiend was just feeling peckish, and the magistrate had been in the wrong place when the dinner bell had rung.

She realized Isabel was looking at her.

"I'm glad you're feeling better," the woman said. "I ... I understand why you took such a fright."

"What? From the werewolves?" asked Deirdre.

"I wasn't sure such things existed."

"No, miss. They do. There are all manner of unexpected things out there."

"Tuppence, thank you for bringing me to the reverend. He seems a wonderful man." There was a hint of uncertainty in Isabel's voice, as if she were more asking a question than making a statement. "And I never got a chance to thank ... you know what, I didn't get the boy's name."

Deirdre wasn't sure what to say. "He ... um ... well, you know those barrow boys, nothing to hold them in one place long."

"Oh, yes, of course." The young woman tilted her head. "Is that singing?"

Deirdre went to the tiny window on the east of their room and peaked out. She immediately went to the door and opened it. The dulcet sound of hymns flooded the room. Even the anvil had stopped. Peering out the open portal, Deirdre saw the Fiend standing on an impromptu podium in the inn yard. He was leading a large assembly in a rousing rendition of "And He Walked Among Us." It was Deirdre's mother's favorite carol. Oddly, rather than raining tears, the young Surrey girl's eyes again rolled in her head.

Isabel soon was in the door beside her. "Oh, wonderful," she whispered. "Such a lovely man."

"There's no one like him," Deirdre agreed.

The hymns and a short sermon afterward (something about forgiving one's neighbors) lasted until the second bell, after which the congregation — which by then numbered several hundred worried locals and Gheet travelers — thanked and congratulated the lean minister. For his part, the Fiend-of-the-cloth invited all to a prayer breakfast he'd arranged at the inn.

As the crowd filed toward the inn's main doors, the Reverend Ainsley approached Isabel and Deirdre. It should have been no surprise to the Surrey girl that the Fiend knew scripture and hymnal so well. He had an enormous library in his tiny cottage, a collection of tomes of which she would have taken advantage were it not for the rage that consumed her.

Still, she would have expected him to whip the crowd into a frothing and angry frenzy. Instead, those still in the courtyard stood in silent contemplation or moved about as if the Blessed Sister herself had just kissed their foreheads. She pursed her lips as the pseudo-padre spoke.

"Ladies, I believe it's safe to leave your room now. The high spirits of the most apprehensive souls have been soothed, and I've taken up a small collection to feed all comers at a prayer breakfast within." He held out an arm to each of the young women, which Deirdre took grudgingly, and escorted them both into the dining hall.

The inn's common room was much larger than those to which Deirdre was accustomed. No fewer than two hundred folks, rich and poor, Gheet and Surrey, were crowded into the chamber, and as the reverend led the two women through the portal, there was a commotion just behind them.

"What's this!" bellowed an enormous man with a face not unlike that of a bull. "I've me lunch and me deputies t'feed! There's evil afoot! Step back, in the name of the law!"

It took only a glance for Deirdre to recognize another Gheet scoundrel — there were oh, so many — and this one was one of the filthiest. Ansel Poutine was the county sheriff and a bane to every hardworking Surrey farmer. A dozen or more times she'd seen the lout at township meetings threatening the victims of felonies and praising their tormentors. A trembling beset her at the sight of the swine, but as disgusting as he was, she knew of no crime the bastard had committed beyond frolicking with the worst of the worst.

She turned and tried her best to ignore the man, but after the preacher found Deirdre and Isabel seats at the room's central table, the skinny fool went and assuaged and pacified the enormous, thick-shanked oaf of a sheriff and offered sheriff and deputies a seat near them at the table.

It was only then that the preacher, to the adoring smiles of all save the sheriff, gave the benediction, a rousing homily on the need to pardon a neighbor's trespasses. Thereafter all assembled jumped into their breakfast feet first. In truth, the food was delightful, but the young woman despised the company. Isabel was on her left and chatted amiably with several of the faithful, the preacher ate like a bird and exchanged sweet glances and pastoral waves with many throughout the room, and the sheriff and his men ate like hungry wolverines, belching, swearing, and grunting all the while.

Several times, the officer glanced at her as if he might know her face, but though Deirdre had the telltale locks and ruddy and freckled complexion of a Surrey, she was clad now as a Gheet lady. The man said nothing, despite the suspicious glances, and continued to stuff his face at an alarming rate.

So swiftly did food vanish from the table that one would have imagined a sideshow conjurer was plying his trade, but then something odd happened. From where he sat at the end of the table, Reverend Ainsley reached with his fork and hooked the final thick slab of bacon from the tray before him. The motion took place a scant moment before the sheriff, who was immediately on the pastor's left, lunged for the same item. Both men, their forks deep within the juicy slab of meat, began a steady and tense tug for the portion. All the while, the churchman's face held a stern but beneficent mien, while the sheriff's mug grew angrier and hotter.

Finally, the Gheet lawman reached out with his nearer hand and gave the good reverend an openhanded clout behind his head, adding a gruff, "leave off, ya' scrawny turnip. A fightin' man needs 'is meat."

The Right Reverend Ainsley gave a rather shocked look, before straightening his clerical collar and resuming his pious posture. He said not a word, and Deirdre again wondered what the Fiend was about. He was being far too nice to everyone, far too nice by half, especially to this lumbering jackass who now wolfed the porcine prize over which the two had tilted.

Deirdre kept her counsel and watched those about her. In no time at all, guests appeared to have taken their fill, but before the first could depart, the pastor rose to his full height, hands folded behind him with great dignity. Clearing his voice, he spoke with a nasal eloquence, his lisp now even more pronounced.

Wergild

"Grandees and gentlefolk, thank you for coming. These are hard times ... hard, *hard* times. And though I do not subscribe to imbibement of spiritous liqueurs and wines, it was the great poet and philosopher Sachet who once said...." The black-clad felon went on that way for some minutes, the assembled apparently leaning on his every word, before he observed that a bit of wine and a skosh of dancing would do no real harm (especially in the morning hours). And he invited those assembled to the same courtyard where hymns previously had been sung so that all might partake in a few drinks and a reel of music and dance or two, "all the better to carry our spirits through these harsh days and to strengthen our resolve to pardon our brothers."

The rush of the assembled to the door could not quite be described as a stampede, but Deirdre soon lost track of the good reverend and soon after that realized Isabel was not to be seen amid the press. She shuffled about for some time, had a short glass of ale, and then wandered into the back of the inn. She'd had no time to interrogate the Fiend since the previous day and wanted to know what he was doing. Passing out the back door, she caught the odor of what could only be the privy closets and turned to leave when she heard a faint splashing in the rear of the property. Something drew her in that direction.

Two dozen paces down a narrow gravel path brought her to the end of a stone building. Rounding that corner, she beheld a sight that caused her to leap once in the air and expel a short and startled shriek.

"Oh, hello, Tuppence," said the reverend as if he didn't have a huge man around the legs plunging him head first into the filthy water of the inn's privy. The man, who it took Deirdre only a moment to realize was the county sheriff, struggled and flailed about pathetically, gasping and choking in the soiled pot as he tried to free himself from the Fiend's iron grip. The Fiend smiled amiably. "I'm in the middle of something right now," he said in a tone a normal person might use to comment on the weather. "It'll be a bit of time. Why don't you...."

Deirdre, who'd stood shocked and staring, unable to utter a word, finally let out a quiet hiss. "*That is not one of my murders!*" She thrust a finger in the direction of the dying Gheet for emphasis.

"Tuppence?" The Fiend seemed surprised.

"You said seven murders," she said with greater vehemence but in a lower whisper. "This one does not count. I want vengeance not you running around butcheri ...."

"Tuppence?" she heard Isabel call out from the inn door through which Deirdre moments before had passed. "Oh! There you are." The Gheet woman began walking down the path at an energetic gait. "I couldn't find you or the reverend and was beginning to worry."

Deirdre began to stutter a response before hearing the Fiend's whispered instructions.

"The two of you meet me at the Congregational Church in New Market. I'll be along later."

Deirdre felt a panic coming on, but she dove into action instead. Striding forward, she met Isabel five paces from the corner behind which the Fiend just had sunk his enormous fangs into the soft upper thighs of the sheriff, whose thrashing by then had all but ceased. Deirdre grabbed Isabel's hand without stopping, very nearly pulling the woman from her feet, and led her back toward the inn door.

It took Isabel several steps to find her balance. "Have you seen Reverend Ainsley?"

"Uh ...," Deirdre began, "he's, um ... he's seeing to a dying parishioner right now and says we should go on to New Market without him. He'll catch up later."

The Gheet woman slowed as they passed through the door. "Is that safe?"

"It'll be fine," said Deirdre, urging the woman on. "It's a short walk, and the roads are busy and well-guarded this time of day." Deirdre's panic was beginning to abate, and something wicked grabbed her tongue. "Besides, the sheriff is nearby."

"Oh, of course," Isabel sighed. "You know, I think Reverend Ainsley is a wonderful man, always on duty, always thinking of others. This world needs more men like him."

"He is a man of great energy," Deirdre couldn't help but agree.

Sloth

"It is a well-known fact that those who are industrious simply have less time to do evil than do the lazy. Thus, is the sad irony of sloth, which really isn't much of a sin."

—***Saint Elsbeth Duck, Abbess of Cubble***

It was late morning when the two travelers, woman and girl, arrived at the Congregational Church in New Market. The day was balmy and kind, and the walk had been remarkably invigorating. Stopping only to refresh themselves from the town fountain, the two spent a short time on the steps of the church chatting amiably about sundry things. Somehow, through it all, Deirdre nearly forgot about the unpleasantness at the inn.

It was less than a quarter bell before Reverend Ainsley joined them on the steps. He arrived in the same high spirits that seemed to be his normal. He was sweetly humming canticles as he approached, and paused with the young ladies for a time, chatting about the virtues of the Walking God and various interpretations of scripture that the morning's walk had taught him.

The man seemed piety quickened into life.

Deirdre was so disarmed by the moment and by the verve of the preacher's soliloquy that she didn't think to be suspicious when he urged her and Isabel to go ahead to a new inn and wait for him there.

"It's been a long and weary trip," he claimed, "and I haven't had time for a proper confession from a senior prelate. If it's all the same, ladies, I'll tarry here and unburden my soul. There's an inn down the High Road, yonder, called the Home of the Seven Saints. The owner is the most devout and delicious woman you could imagine." The cleric slid Deirdre a small purse. "I'll be along shortly."

It took the entire walk from the church to the inn for Deirdre to pull the wool from off her eyes. What had she been thinking? The Fiend wasn't going for confession, communion, or any other rite. She and Isabel already were at the inn and sitting at a booth in the dining hall before Deirdre began swearing under her breath.

"Tuppence!" was the young Gheet woman's shocked whisper.

"Oh, sorry. I just forgot something I needed to tell Reverend Ainsley. You don't mind waiting here until I return? It shouldn't be more than two shakes of a duck's tail."

The young lass had by then already snaked out of the booth, and Isabel gave her a kind smile and a nod. Dashing out the door and striding up the street, Deirdre continued to scold herself. Really, what had she been thinking? If she reached the church and found.... She made a guttural sound and picked up her pace.

She made it to the church in half the time it took her and Isabel to walk from it, and when she pulled open the nearest of the two great double doors that were the enormous structure's front entrance, she should not have been surprised by what she saw. But she was, deeply.

Within the church, she beheld a balding old fat man bent double over the central altar, and he was as naked as the day he was born. Behind the now purple-faced and pathetically gagging and whimpering man was the Fiend, his hands gripped hard around some sturdy cloth he was using as a garrote to throttle his hapless victim.

When she spoke, it was in a voice choked with she knew not what. "*I cannot leave you alone for even a minute!*" She didn't know why she said that. They were the only words that seemed to leap to mind.

"Ah, Tuppence. Hello again. Could you close the door?"

Throughout, the Fiend's fat victim continued to choke and squeal, and several incoherent gurgling noises now emanated from him that may have been attempts to beg mercy.

Deirdre ignored them, but by reflex reached back and pulled the door closed. The streets weren't crowded, but neither were they empty. What if someone walked in at that moment? The Fiend hadn't even thought to bar the door. Her ire finally bested her shock and fear.

"Will you stop that!" she hissed as quietly as her temper permitted.

"What?"

"I...!" she began to shout.

"Oh, very well...," said the Fiend, adopting a conciliatory tone, after which his mouth distended, and in one swift move he locked his huge fangs onto the gurgling and choking man's neck, twisted once to a cracking sound, and leapt to the ceiling twenty feet above, where he swiftly used the cloth garrote to hang the now lifeless corpse from the central rafter.

As he dropped to the floor, the reverend, now more Fiend than clergyman, reached out with the claw of a single finger and pricked the naked corpse's great belly. A long and lean slither of intestines followed the Fiend to the ground. It took many seconds for the entire intestinal ribbon, foot after foot of the grisly stuff, to slide out the belly and onto the floor, during which the Fiend danced and capered about muttering every sort of obscenity and hooting a cacophony of ecclesiastical mumbo jumbo.

Even after all the Fiend had shown her, the lunacy of that moment left Deirdre trembling and speechless, especially after the Fiend crouched down and began sucking in enormous mouthfuls of intestines.

It finally was too much, and the mortified young woman had to resist the urge to retch before she spoke.

"Will you stop that! We have to go! What if someone walks in!?" She didn't want to get closer than necessary, but the urge just to grab him nearly overcame her.

Before she did, he relented.

The Fiend, now suddenly Reverend Ainsley again, rose and spoke in a voice that was more sad than peevish. "Oh, very well, Tuppence ... though I had planned on taking this time to compose a sermon on the sin of sloth. It was a half bell past second, and this terrible man wouldn't rouse himself from bed to take my confession. And him a bishop, nonetheless!"

"How could that possibly...?" began a now near hysterical Deirdre.

"Can you imagine," said the reverend, who somehow hadn't a speck of blood or viscera on his perfect collar or overcoat, "the bastard dared give me a cuff upside the head for even asking him to take my confession at a time set by ecclesiastical law for the sacrament. The sacrilege." The faux reverend moved in a dignified step toward the door. A faint smile played at his handsome mouth when he opened the great portal and gracefully motioned Deirdre to take the lead.

Outside, she began to run, but a boney hand slowed her.

"Never run from a crime scene, Tuppence," were the gentle and pastoral words of the learned minister. "It only draws attention."

The two continued on at a casual pace for some minutes, Deirdre aching to bolt and run or to start screaming at every step of it. The reverend hummed peacefully, even gayly, a phenomenon that increased the farther they traveled from the great church. By the time three blocks had passed, she was fairly certain the Fiend at any moment would break into song and dance.

"What are you so happy about?" the trembling lass whispered without looking in his direction, as if doing so would draw attention to them.

The reverend began to giggle in a very unecclesiastical fashion. He gave a deep sigh. "The chitlins of a fat man of fifty years' age." Another sigh. "If I had nothing else to eat for the rest of my long and miserable life, breakfast, lunch, and dinner, I would never tire of such a feast."

Deirdre finally looked up at him, no longer trying to hide her shock.

"So sweet," he went on, "so delectable. You know the trick, Tuppence? You have to start with the testicles and work your way up. It gives the fresh chitlins a tang that can never be captured through any spice or sauces."

By that time, they were nearly halfway to the inn, and the street was empty, but it would not have mattered. Deirdre let out an angry and frightened yelp.

"What?" he asked in surprise.

"How? What? ... back there?" She was flummoxed. True, the man the Fiend had throttled and eaten clearly was a Gheet, and a Gheet clergyman at that. That he was dead, and was killed in front of her, bothered her only a little. Well, more than a little. But the Fiend's random snacking was getting them nowhere! She finally mustered her thoughts. "Do you have any sort of plan?!"

Reverend Ainsley stopped and drew himself to his full height. There was no hint of anger on his face, but his voice had just a trace of emotion. "Tuppence, have I ever come to your farm and told you how to farm? ... No? Then please do not ever tell me how to fiend. Now, I don't have a *full* plan yet, but I do have a plan. And I'll do my very best to do right by you. I give you my word."

"The word of a fiend?"

"The word of a friend." He lay his hand on her shoulder. "I am your friend, aren't I? Do you trust me to do my best for you?"

A tear seized her eye, and she gave a short nod. She'd seen how he was with people, how he manipulated them. But at that moment, she didn't care if he was doing it to her. She needed this, she needed it so badly.

His arm still on her shoulder, he resumed walking, pulling her close as he did. She walked beside him as a daughter might with a father.

Wergild

He patted her shoulder after they'd strolled a way. "I'm sorry if my dining choices upset you. You've seen how I eat at the barrow, lots of cauliflower and cucumbers ... maybe a nibble of fish when the stream is running." His voice became apologetic. "I don't eat people every day. Not even every year. I have a nice slice of fat man maybe once every fifteen or twenty years. Is that alright?"

"Yeah," she grumbled. Her tone was grudging, but she really didn't feel that way. "As long as they're Gheets."

"I'll try to stick to that diet," he replied.

A few minutes later, they reached the inn and found Isabel happily waiting.

―――

Isabel wasn't certain how to take Tuppence. At times, the young womanchild was amiable and playful, and at others morose and sullen. All throughout, Isabel sensed in the girl a deep and seething anger, as if some great and irredeemable wrong had been done her. Then Isabel remembered how she herself had been at fourteen and cut the kid a break. Isabel's life at that age hardly had been roses, and she hadn't been raised in the coarse and violent world in which she now found herself. If Tuppence had issues, she probably had a right to them.

Little time had passed since breakfast, but both she and Tuppence were hungry, so they pondered what to eat. Reverend Ainsley calmly abstained from dining, but if there truly was a man who needed to bulk up, it was him. Handsome he may have been — and he had an otherworldly charm and charisma — but he was as thin as a fencepost.

There were no proper menus, but on the wall, a thick slate signaled the fare of the day. Her understanding of the language was strong, but the script still often evaded her. Pointing to some glyphs at the top of the placard, she asked her companions what they meant.

"Chitlins," Tuppence snarled.

Was there a hint of disgust in the girl's voice? No matter. Isabel instead smiled. "We have those at home. Pigs intestines, right?"

"Oh, here they can come from the innards of most any animal," replied the reverend in a mild and sage tone. "But I'd recommend the chicken. It is truly delightful. And think not at all of payment. Sir Alexis has generously deposed me with funds to tide us during travel."

"That is very generous, reverend. Thank you." She couldn't keep a smile from crossing her face. "And I wish Sir Alexis was here, so I might tell him the same."

"He's not the kind of man who needs thanks," added Tuppence, this time with a sincere smile. "He's not a big talker, either. And he's particular about what he eats."

It took Isabel a moment to think whether she'd missed some subtext of Tuppence's words. By that time, the reverend had communicated their desires to a handsome woman of some forty years who appeared to be the proprietress.

"Wait, reverend. Are you sure you won't eat anything?"

"Oh, Lady Isabel, I draw my sustenance from other sources. And mortification of the flesh is a central tenant of our religious faith. One cannot grow closer to the divine while adhering to the base slavery of the *corpus*. For me, food is a necessity of which I partake only *in extremis*."

"Tell me about your religion, reverend." She suddenly was hungry for knowledge she'd hesitated to discuss with Sir Utrecht. It seemed important now.

Over the next half hour, as they awaited their meal, the pastor talked about the great beings in their world, the Walking God, a force for justice and good, and the "Other One," a being so evil and malevolent that most deigned not to give it a name. It was all very Manichean, with the force of good, as described by the reverend, sounding very much like a great and mischievous Santa Claus, but one living its divine existence swathed in the humble guise of a common human, living and working among mortal folk as one of them, always ready to step in and right wrongs done to others. The Walking God was both common man and a trickster, a mercurial character who showed many faces and who often meted out rough justice by cunning and guile.

It was all very touching as told by a learned Doctor of Religion, but Isabel couldn't help but have her doubts. True, she'd seen wonderous things since her arrival in Albion, a world completely different from her own Earth. But a god who walked among people and served justice through wiliness and trickery seemed to be nothing more than a story that explained every simple coincidence. She'd always imagined herself a rational and reasonable person. This all sounded like storytelling designed to quiet a frightened child, or to give hope to adults when there was none.

Wergild

But she smiled and said nothing, only paying particular attention to the minor theological differences between the various Surrey and Gheet denominations, ones that the reverend warned the parties were especially prickly about enforcing. It had been some years since the last heretic had been burned for referring to the "Walking God" as the "God who Walked," but some remained particularly wedded to that subtle yet vital distinction.

After their food was served, the two young women ate in contented silence while the pastor struck up a conversation with the proprietress, Mrs. Villeneuve, a pretty and shapely Gheet woman with a sweet and pious way about her. The two spoke at some length about ecclesiastical nuance so subtle that after scant minutes Isabel understood none of it. Not long after, the reverend arranged for a room for Isabel and Tuppence, and he and Mrs. Villeneuve repaired to the inn's chapel to consult scripture.

This left Isabel alone with Tuppence, whose spirits seemed to have improved since her return with the reverend. When first the two had entered the inn, Tuppence had been in an emotional state. Though the girl didn't seem truly angry, had Isabel not known better, she would have thought Tuppence and the reverend had quarreled.

But how unlikely would such a development be? The reverend was the most modest and self-effacing of men and looked upon the girl with such gentle eyes. It was that notion that most convinced Isabel of the deep worth of Tuppence. Every person Isabel had seen in company with the young lass — Sir Alexis, the boy, and now Reverend Ainsley — had regarded her with such tenderness, even though she was so often cranky and morose.

Still, the young woman provided amiable company that evening in the common room and later in their chambers, a tiny room in the servants' area of the otherwise full inn. Isabel learned much about life on the farm and the perils of being a Surrey in times such as these. Tuppence was unusually pleasant and generous with her smiles, and the two passed the first pleasant evening that Isabel had known in many days.

Until the howling began.

Greed

"This sin is the one that will send you straight to Hell.
Greed is the worst of them, worse even than lust. For at least lust wanes with the passing of years and the graying of the temple, but a man's greed grows more frenzied as he ages.
For the true sinner, there can never be enough, until every halfpenny drags him into the Inferno."
—**Dr. Erasmus Pertwee, Dean of Theology and Eschatology,**
Kings College, Portsmouth

Deirdre came to the painful conclusion that Isabel was daft.
She didn't like to think of her new friend in that way. The woman was beautiful, tall, and stately and had a heart of gold. But she often was at a loss for words, could barely read, and still was not married in her middle twenties, an age at which most women, both Surrey and Gheet, had been wed ten years or more. Worse, she often seemed confused by even the simplest of things. Clearly there was some defect that wasn't obvious.

Just moments before, as they'd awaited the preacher in the courtyard outside the inn, Isabel completely had missed the import of an unfortunate and short-tempered jibe Deirdre had made.

It all had begun late the evening before, when an audible howling and grunting had erupted from somewhere nearby. Deirdre had been raised on a large family farm. The sound of animals rutting, both human and barnyard, was as familiar to her as a sparrow's cry. So, she'd promptly rolled over and gone to sleep.

But the nature and provenance of the feral howls and growls, which were still discernable until just before dawn, had seemed a frightening mystery to Isabel. When the woman finally had found the gumption to inquire about them, Deirdre, still a bit cranky without her breakfast, had grumbled that it was the demon getting its exercise — she really needed to mind her tongue — a statement to which a much-relieved Isabel had replied that the correct word was "exorcise," before going on to further extol the virtues of the Right Reverend Moorcroft Ainsley.

"Are such things common hereabouts?" Isabel asked even now.

"Uhh ... I'm sorry?" It took Deirdre a moment to realize what she was being asked.

"Exorcisms. Are those common hereabouts?"

"Oh ... uh," Deirdre didn't know what to say until she saw the reverend walking down the outside staircase from the inn's second floor, a brown package in his hand and a disheveled Mrs. Villeneuve waving a hasty goodbye behind him. Deirdre gave the woman a moment to slip back indoors. "Oh, you should ask the reverend. Here he comes."

The cheerful, almost gleeful, look of the minister seemed to put Isabel off for a moment. When she began to ask about the reverend's nocturnal doings, he corrected her.

"Ah, one of the lesser known rites of our faith. The good landlady and I were attempting to speak in tongues, so as to channel the *animus* of the Walking God's nature spirit." He smiled sweetly. "Truly, it can be disconcerting for the uninitiated."

By that time, he was leading the two women out onto the road, where he produced from the package he carried some bread, cheese, and lovely summer sausage. They talked more as they ambled westward, the reverend occasionally greeting passersby or uttering sweet benedictions to the faithful as they went. The locals were nothing but smiles for the amiable murderer and lecher.

"At this time of year," the reverend informed them as they neared the town's western gate, "we should have no trouble hitching a ride on a cargo wagon heading west. Most go that way empty after discharging their cargo along the coast and are happy to make a few farthings hauling anything or anyone."

It was no surprise that the three travelers soon comfortably were seated on the back of a hay wagon headed for the town of Gatsby, the county seat, which was near where Isabel hoped to find Sir Brian Mayfield and where the preacher informed them that they might likewise encounter Sir Alexis de Vere.

"The trip is more than a day, so we may need to find shelter along the road. But that's no problem. Inns are plentiful and reasonable, and this has always been a peaceful land."

For the Gheets, Deirdre nearly said aloud. But she tempered her words. There was no use correcting the Fiend. He knew what the two of them were truly about. At least *he* did — Deirdre still wasn't certain. The road rolled by, and sometime in midmorning Lady Isabel was snoozing easily in the hay. Deirdre took that opportunity to feed her curiosity.

"Is any of what you said the other day true?" she asked the Fiend.

"What's that, Tuppence?"

"You know what I mean." She took a painful swallow and hesitated a moment. "Is there really a Walking God?"

It was the first earnest surprise she'd seen on any of the Fiend's faces. "Of course, there is ... after a fashion."

"Nooo ...," she howled in a tiny voice. "Be honest for once."

"I am being honest," he replied. "Such a being does exist. But it's no god. At least not in the sense you think of one."

"But ... if he ... it isn't a god?"

The Fiend actually took a long look around and even peeked at Isabel to make sure she truly slept. None could hear them. "There are a great many things those in power don't want the people to know. This is one. Once, great ages ago, this world of yours was a battlefield. Two grand tribes — godly tribes if you want to call them that, beings of unimaginable power — each claimed this world as their own. They fought over it for a very long time, until both sides realized that should that fight continue, they surely would destroy this world that each so greatly admired."

"This world? Our world?" she interjected.

"Oh, yes. It's a lovely and pristine world in which you live. The people aren't perfect, but where isn't that true? ... But I digress. In short, the two warring parties both agreed to depart this world, but to ensure the peace, each left a guardian ... a warden of sorts, whose job it is to make sure the other side doesn't transgress the treaty and seize this world for themselves."

"And that's the Walking God?"

"Yes. But the rest is just a charade. This being of which you speak plays no role in your world. It's part of the agreement between the two warring sides. Neither guardian is allowed to interfere directly in human affairs. It would violate the treaty if they did. This 'Walking God' is just a fiction drummed up by those who supported one side of the war, and they tarred the guardian from the other side with an uglier brush. Truth is, neither of them really does much, but waits and watches. The people in this lovely world could get to blazes for all this alleged Walking God cares."

"There are no forces of good and evil in our world ... like they say in scripture?" Her words weren't truly a question. It was more something she'd already sensed.

"No, Deirdre. There are good and bad beings. You see them every day in the world in which you live."

"Us ... people, I mean?"

"Yes," he nodded.

"And fiends?"

"Oh, yes. There are all manner of beings — fiends, bogies, ogres, trolls, and many more — all left behind by the two tribes when they left this world. Some tend more toward brutal and cruel ways than others, but the worst such creatures, fiends included, are no eviler than the worst men and women."

"I believe that." She nodded and beamed a great smile. He'd called her Deirdre. "How do you know all of that, the bit about the gods? Oh, wait. It's the wind, isn't it?"

He smiled. "Partly the wind, but I also read. There are many things a body can learn from reading books."

It was true. Books. The Fiend's cottage had been awash with them. "I should have read some of those," she grumbled.

"It's never too late, Tuppence. A book is a friend that doesn't judge us for our neglect and that always greets us warmly when we return."

They passed most of the remains of the day in silence, talking only of minor things when they felt the need, and the three ended up taking a room at the Wayfarer Inn some miles short of Gatsby. There appeared to be some sort of tournament farther west, and the reverend claimed they would have a difficult time finding a room inside the city walls. The place was near enough that they'd still make the town early the next morning.

No sooner did the reverend see the young women ensconced in their small but comfortable room at the Wayfarer than he excused himself to "look in on the penitent and weary." Isabel gave an amiable smile, but Deirdre knew something was afoot. The scallywag was up to something, and she intended to know what.

After a short delay, she excused herself to Lady Isabel, who stayed to bathe and rest, and followed the hallway to the stairs and down to the common room. Not ten minutes had passed since Moorcroft Ainsley had left them, but he was nowhere to be seen in the great room, which already held fifty or more patrons, eating, drinking, and gaming. Clearly, the Fiend was again about his antics and had shed one face for yet another.

She just needed to find that face.

There were several false starts as she espied patrons who she thought were the Fiend only to realize as a hand rested on an unwelcome part of her body that the man in question thought her an eager serving girl or a local sporting lady. One such episode ended with her leaping in the air with a high-pitched squeak.

Hanging about the common rooms of inns and watching games of chance was scarcely a lady-like endeavor, but before she could embarrass herself further, she heard a loud and sharp voice from a table farthest from the door. The sound came from a slight but energetic man of about forty years. His back was to the wall, and he was in the midst of some type of card game with five other men. He called out again.

"Miss, I'll give you a tuppence, if you fetch me an ale."

It was a pittance for a human soul, but a hefty sum for fetching a drink. The Fiend's sense of humor had not left him, and she went to the bar, recovered an ale, and took it to the man. Before she could say or do anything further, the man pointed to a chair behind him.

"You're my lucky token now, missy." He smiled. "I'll call you Tuppence if you don't mind."

She took her pennies and her seat and began to watch.

Chance Medley was a reprobate and a gambler, and over the next several hours, the man smoked, drank, cursed, and emptied the purses of at least six other men, six very angry and ugly Gheets. Though pleasant and affable, Chance didn't even pretend at humility. As the evening drew to a close, he made a great show of counting his winnings, laughing up his good fortune, and pointing out that he would be taking the High Road east to his camp, alone, on a night following at least three vicious and gory murders.

"Ha!" Chance barked. "I've got a sharp knife and a fleet foot for a man my age. Does anyone seriously believe the magistrate and the others were killed by anyone but highwaymen or some sour Surrey rebel? If anyone wants to rob me, they can kiss my ass. I absolutely refuse to spit up a penny of my money ... you gentlemen's money," he grinned wickedly, "to some thug just 'cause he's got a pig sticker." Chance then laughed like a man thrice his size and levered himself from the chair in which he sat. He swayed gently, as a man well into his cups might.

Deirdre was mortified. The Fiend was taunting these men to follow him out and ... and there were five of them. No, six. But he was a fiend, wasn't he? What could even six grown men do against a fiend? She was beset by indecision. She worried for the Fiend. He was her ally, the only one she had. But none of these men had given her offense. True, each had the cocky demeanor and condescending voice typical of a filthy Gheet — any one of them could have been among those who'd so callously, but ... but....

A battle raged within her. There was a core decency and goodness within Deirdre that desperately was at odds with the fury and anger that of late had guided her every thought and action. She wanted blood and vengeance and had bristled at the Fiend's earlier inaction, but part of her was horrified at the campaign of culinary carnage the creature now carried out.

What had these men done? She hoped her friend had a plan, but didn't know, not really. Even if he taunted these men for a good purpose, how many things might go wrong? He was just one fiend. What if...? What if...?

By that time, Chance Medley had pulled on his jaunty blue coat and made his unsteady way to the exit, turning only once to give her a quick wink and a roll of the eyebrows. And then he was out the door.

The men who'd gamed with him were at first silent, and then the swearing began, low and angry. Deirdre made herself absent, taking up a seat beyond the bar on the far side of the room. But as she watched and strained to listen, the anger and fury of the men grew slowly in volume before dropping suddenly into conspiratorial whispers. It took the men some time, but after more cursing and no few ales, they rose as one and headed for the door. They now were silent, save for the portly fiftyish man who appeared to be their leader — the evening boded ill for that one — who ordered one man, the oldest and frailest among them, to stay behind.

Deirdre counted to fifty before she followed the men out the door. It was full dark by that time, and the echo of the men's voices and the scant light of their lantern was still clear along the road to the east. She tarried only a moment to allow her eyes to adjust and then tore off after them at a run.

Fortunately, the land along that stretch of the High Road was clear but for some low brush and brambles. Deirdre was able to make her way around the men, who proceeded at a steady walk, and soon was racing along a cow path parallel with the road. It took far longer than she wanted, but she soon spied a figure in the murk who could only be Chance Medley, the Fiend. Another few minutes passed as she picked her way through a patch of bushes and reached his side. By that time, she was too winded to speak.

"Tuppence," said the gambler with a smile, "what a pleasant surprise. What brings you out on such an evening?"

She raised her hand as if to speak but instead leaned forward on her knees to catch her breath.

"It took our friends long enough to find their courage," he continued. "I'm assuming that's why you're here…?"

"Five of them," she finally was able to huff out. "Five of them…."

The Fiend leapt in the air and promptly began to cut a jig near the base of a large oak beside the High Road. He giggled hysterically. "I'd expected two or maybe three … but five! … Woohoo!"

Her breath finally came to her. "You're not worried? They have knives and cudgels."

The Fiend calmed himself and gave her an indulgent smile. "Tuppence, you are a delight … hold on." He turned his head as if to listen. "Up in the tree with you. Quick."

She felt herself suddenly weightless, and the lower branch of the great oak was even with her face. The Fiend's strong hands lifted her farther, and she grabbed on and scampered into the tree.

"A little higher," he whispered. "And don't make a sound."

By that time, the noisy and bellicose speech of the approaching men was clear even to Deirdre's hearing. The Gheet were loud, loud in that way only frightened men felt the need to be, and it was some minutes before they came fully into view.

"Chance Medley," called out their leader, as if in surprise. It seemed they intended to make a game of it. "What is the chance we'd find you here?"

Only two of the man's drunken lackeys laughed at his pitiful attempt at humor, probably because the others either were too nervous or too stupid to understand the silly jape.

Chance swayed up to the men amiably, as if still under the influence of too much ale. "Why, hello ... what was your name again?"

That was too much for the seething bully, and he drew back and struck Chance hard in the face. Two others rushed in and tackled the gambler and began pummeling him mercilessly. A fourth stepped up and kicked the now prostrate man hard in the ribs after which he took a cudgel to his lower back. Throughout, their victim made hardly a noise, but he did manage to wriggle free, spring to his feet, and face the five men, fists raised as if ready to box.

But the men began to circle him warily, smiling and laughing all the while. Now that they'd landed their first cowardly blows, their fear appeared to have dissipated. Only one, the youngest of the bunch, lagged behind.

"What about you?" Chance called out to the young man. "Your pappy here holding your balls for you?"

The younger man did indeed favor the ringleader, and he stepped forward now, his face ashen but bellicose. The youth wasn't too many years older than Deirdre, and for just the barest of moments, her resolve abandoned her.

"Don't do it!" she cried out in a voice so emotional it came out as barely a peep. "He's a fiend!"

All eyes went to where Deirdre was concealed in the tree, and after the briefest silence, one of the attackers spoke up.

"Well, damn, Marcus, I guess you're popping both your cherries tonight!"

The scoundrels broke into a sick laughter, but the Fiend cast another hidden wink and affectionate smile to Deirdre in her perch. A moment later, having found his courage, Marcus threw a haymaker at Chance's face.

The young fool's fist landed inside the Fiend's now gaping maw, and after the briefest of moments to let the terror sink home, the Fiend bore down with his fangs and whipped his head three times, ripping off the youngster's arm at the shoulder. The erstwhile prey then shot like a bolt for the soft flesh beneath the leader's belly and, after lifting that man from the ground as he once had the magistrate, repeated the furious agitation that moments before had disarmed the son.

For the next ten minutes, chaos reigned as the Fiend ran amok like a weasel in a henhouse, slashing, ripping, chewing, and dismembering the five men. Only one attempted to flee and was stopped when the Fiend, his fangs still deep in the belly of another ruffian, snatched up a dagger and made a lazy underhand toss into the fleeing man's lower back, dropping the fugitive in a heap.

It simply was dreadful, but Deirdre was unable to avert her gaze. Her heart was torn between glee and terror, and she found herself shaking, not from the brutal violence without, but from her own deep conflict within.

The Fiend made short work of the men, and the havoc was over as quickly as it had begun. By that time, Deirdre already was making her shaky descent from the great tree, and it took her several tries before she toppled out awkwardly into a nearby bush. A now smiling and perfectly composed Chance fished her out.

"You really shouldn't have come," he said in a quiet tone as he picked leaves and twigs from her hair.

"I ... you...." She let out a growl. "I wanted to know what you were up to. And ... and ... those don't count toward my seven," she said, making a perfunctory gesture to the unsightly patch of disarticulated ruffians beside the High Road. She wasn't feeling feverish as she had after the first night's carnage, but now a great weakness rushed over her. Without thinking, she leaned against Chance, who swept her up into his arms and began to saunter back in the general direction of the Wayfarer Inn.

"I'm sorry I cried out like I did," she whispered against the top of his shoulder.

"It was no bother."

"They never really had a chance, did they?"

He began to laugh quietly. "They took a Chance, but it didn't turn out the way they wanted."

It wasn't very funny, so she didn't laugh. She asked a question instead. "Why?"

"You mean, why those men?"

She nodded in his arms.

"They were Gheets. Hasn't that always been enough for you?"

"I don't know," she answered after several false starts.

"I'm still working on my plan, Tuppence, refining the rougher edges. I promise to tell you the minute I've worked out the kinks. Until then, your concern for your fellow humans does you great credit, even if they were five murderous lowlifes."

Wergild

His final words left her feeling oddly satisfied. She still was too weak to walk on her own, and when they returned to the inn some minutes later, the Fiend — once again sporting the guise of Moorcroft Ainsley — took her to the now unoccupied public baths. He fetched some lukewarm water to cool her body, and while she bathed, he sat with his back to her and carefully picked the burrs and thistles from her dress and britches. Afterward, he turned slightly and helped her with her hair, averting his gaze all the while and speaking only to speculate whether some warm buttermilk might not settle a sudden case of indigestion.

It was late when she returned to her room, and creeping inside she found Isabel fast asleep. Deirdre didn't know what tomorrow would bring. It was all such a jumble and a mess. But it likely would entail someone getting eaten, an eventuality that she now decided she could accept.

Wrath

"Every man sees his own anger as being perfectly justified. That's the bait which makes wrath the trickiest and most seductive of all the sins."
—**Brother Constance**

Isabel awoke early the next morning to the sound of voices, singing voices raised in praise. It was delightful, but coming as it did before dawn's first light, the timing might have been better. Twice more before she finally lifted her blankets and began her day, the honeyed and precious sound of hymns and the cultured lilt of Reverend Ainsley's preaching left her feeling a little peevish for lack of proper sleep.

It wasn't until she ventured downstairs that she discovered the cause of the early-morning sermonizing. The local prosecutor — a man of unquestioned decency and probity — along with the prosecutor's son and three others, had been murdered and dismembered by a lycanthrope not one mile from the inn, and the local populace was near panic. It was ghastly, simply horrible.

But at the center of this raging maelstrom was the tall, lean, and stalwart form of Right Reverend Moorcroft Ainsley, a steady hand at the tiller, a voice of courage in the dark, a man of faith and reason preaching of love and forgiveness.

By the time Isabel had made her way from the room she shared with Tuppence, it was an hour past dawn and the reverend already had preached three sermons. She found the angular clergyman in the courtyard, speaking in reassuring tones, waving benedictions to smiling parishioners, and filling the place with hope. Isabel had never been much for religion in her old life, but Reverend Ainsley was such a decent, pious, and godly man. The world, this world and her old, needed more men like him.

She now felt a little guilty for having awoken in such a bad temper, a notion that only compounded the shame she felt over the peculiar thoughts that earlier had sprung to mind over what the reverend actually had been up to with Mrs. Villeneuve in New Market. Honestly, having grown up in

Wergild

the American South, one would expect her to have a better opinion of ministers.

Swallowing her guilt, she left the reverend to his duties and sought out Tuppence, who she found in the common room with her nose buried in a book, an item Isabel learned the reverend had gifted her that very morning. (It was something about a girl who beguiles a dragon.) The two young women spoke briefly, and as Isabel awaited her breakfast, she attempted to coax Tuppence into further conversation.

"I'm sorry I retired before you returned last night," she began. She gave the reticent young woman a moment to reply and then continued. "Did the reverend need your help with something?"

Tuppence lay down her book. "He didn't exactly need my help, but I felt I needed to be there."

"Oh," Isabel replied. Tuppence for all her moodiness was still the very heart of goodness. "Do you think I might help the reverend in some small way?"

For some reason a blank look flashed across Tuppence's face, followed by a tiny smile. "You should ask him," was all the Surrey girl said.

Before Isabel could form another thought, there was a great commotion in the courtyard, followed by a tremendous shout.

"Fornicator!"

Isabel was shocked and horrified at the scene she and Tuppence found in the courtyard. Moments before, there had been a series of shouts of "fornicator" and "adulterer" in the yard, and when she and Tuppence had gone to investigate, they'd found a half dozen men, swords in hand, facing the good Reverend Ainsley. The man at their center, upon whom Isabel had never laid eyes, continued to shout.

He was accusing Reverend Ainsley of having taken unnatural and depraved advantage of the man's wife. It wasn't until she heard the man's name, Villeneuve, that she began to color and bite her lip. Certainly not. Certainly, her own perverse imaginings couldn't have been true. There no doubt was something pompous and maybe even a little unctuous about the reverend, but she was as sure as the sky was blue that he wouldn't engage in any such base and immoral depravity. The man starved himself of every pleasure life had to offer.

The answer was obvious. The same set of silly coincidences that had led Isabel to her momentary and shameless suspicion must have been latched onto by someone who didn't know the reverend. In this world, as in her own, rumors had a life of their own — though in Albion the results were far deadlier. This realization only deepened her shame at having participated in such a farce, even if only in her own heart.

As she stepped forward to intercede, a strong hand gripped her arm and pulled her back. Tuppence.

The young girl shook her head. "There's no interfering, Lady Isabel."

With a feeble cry, Isabel's hands flew to her mouth. She knew the girl was right. The telltale reddening of the minister's left cheek said it all. The man, Villeneuve, had struck Reverend Ainsley across the face before she and Tuppence had arrived. A blood duel was the only reply to such an affront.

Something began to grow in her, a fear, a terror, an enormous sense of dread and loss. Its source was clear, and it was an overwhelming sensation that caused her body to tremble and her knees to feel weak. What sort of world was this? First it took fair Sir Utrecht, her first friend and only protector, and now sweet and pious Reverend Ainsley. What would that man know about wielding a sword? This was a land that found the best and purest and sought to grind them to nothing.

Somehow, she found herself back at the table where minutes before she'd been with Tuppence. The young Surrey lass had taken up her book and appeared to be leafing through, as if attempting to discern where she'd left off. What kind of people were these? Even Tuppence!

"This is no time to read!" She snapped those words and regretted them instantly, but before she could apologize, she saw a look on the face of Tuppence. Had the youngster just rolled her eyes?

Tuppence sighed and began to speak. "Lady Isabel, this is the way of things. But don't fret. Among the common folk and lower gentry, there's hardly ever a fight to the death. Most likely, someone will get poked or cut up a tad. And besides...." The girl seemed to grope for words. "Those skinny ones are a lot slipperier than you'd think. Ah, um ... a wiry fella like the preacher will prove himself just fine."

As if in afterthought, Tuppence scooted a short way down the bench they shared and awkwardly placed her arm around Isabel, cradling the woman's head on her shoulder and no doubt, Isabel suspected, rolling her eyes all the while.

Wergild

All Deirdre wanted was to find out whether the beryl stone in the necklace would summon the ether dragon or the frost drake, but every time her eyes strayed to the new book Reverend Ainsley had given her, she felt Lady Isabel's cold and disapproving gaze upon her. Deirdre wished there was some way she could inform the anxious and frightened woman that there was nothing about which she needed to worry. The fix was in. And she needn't agonize over burying another friend. By all rights, Robert Villeneuve was an accomplished duelist, but he had about as much chance of besting the tall and gangly reverend as he had of sprouting wings and flying.

Though she knew it not, Isabel's protector was as safe as a bug in a rug. But it would be a short while before the young woman found that out.

Under some ancient writ, a duel between commoners could not be fought until two bells had passed after the challenge, and even now, as Villeneuve warmed up his fencing arm in the field yonder, the Fiend was over in same said field, overegging the pudding. Reverend Ainsley's pious devotions, which at first had been amusing, even touching, now were getting a little monotonous. How many confessions could he take? How many blessings could he bestow? How many benedictions, benisons, orisons, prayers, and supplications?

How many prayer chains could he start, fervently praying for Robert Villeneuve's immortal soul? In front of the crowd, and it was a crowd of almost carnivalesque proportion that awaited the duel, the good reverend was acting like the cuckold Villeneuve was the victim of some grotesque injustice — which he in fact was, in several deeply ironic ways, but *no one* other than Deirdre and the Fiend knew that. Only they two knew for certain Mayor Villeneuve — for he was mayor of the local township — was a dead man.

There was a smidge of curiosity in Deirdre about how the Fiend would pull it off, whether the reverend would get in one lucky swipe or whether Mayor Villeneuve would accidently fall on his own sword. Truth was, she had no guess how the man's death would come to pass, but there was no question the Right Reverend Ainsley would come out smelling like a rose.

She found herself smiling and bit her lip to stop. Glancing up, she caught sight of a tremulous and pale Isabel standing near the great oak under which combat was soon to commence. The poor thing looked a nervous wreck, and Deirdre did want to ease her worry in some way. But the Surrey lass just wasn't good at acting and was unable to veil her indifference, a shortcoming which had rendered her earlier attempts to comfort her companion somewhat counterproductive.

Deirdre just couldn't bring herself to put on a face she didn't feel and instead sat bored, deeply bored.

She thought of just grabbing the book and dashing upstairs for a few undisturbed pages of reading — the tome cried out to her from where it rested on a satchel to her right — but that would only aggravate the Isabel problem. No, she had to pretend to ... oh ... to do what?!

She leaned back in the soft grass, and it occurred to her that there was some method to all this. The Fiend hadn't said he was *without* a plan. He said he was without a *full* plan. So there had to be something there, some reason or rhyme for why ... well, why he was about to skewer the good mayor. If truth be told, she hadn't really thought about why the Fiend had turned his attentions to Mrs. Villeneuve two nights before (nor why he'd been so flagrant in doing so — they'd kept half the inn awake with their clamorous coupling), and it hadn't seemed appropriate to ask. Now it was obvious. The creature was looking for a reason to inter the woman's husband.

She found herself frowning.

Why would he need a reason? He'd always before just pounced. Perhaps the good Lady Villeneuve had been available when the husband was not? Hmm.... No. Couldn't the so-called reverend have waited for the man? Or gone looking for him? They weren't exactly on a time schedule ... were they?

She cleared her head and frowned more deeply.

Hullo, she thought. First the magistrate in the road, then the sheriff in the privy, then the bishop in the ... well, not the belfry, but that sounded good, and then the prosecutor under the oak. And now the township mayor under a different oak.

"Damn," she whispered to no one.

Why those men? The slaughter had seemed random at first, since the fools simply popped up along the way as she and the Fiend had travelled, but why Gheet officials? Now it seemed less random, and she wondered how the Fiend knew each would be in just the right place to do his nasty bit of work on them.

Wergild

The wind? She'd really never pressed him on what that meant, but it was the Fiend's frequent reply to how he knew things he ought not. The wind told him.

Okay, set that aside. *Why those men?*

She never knew the names of those murders, thieves, and rapists who'd victimized her family and friends, but she could name twice two-score Gheet families who were the worst tormentors of the Surrey in Edwin Township. Like as not, you could kill at random any seven men from any of those families and be sure to send at least one murderer to Hell.

But why Gheet grandees and not those men? Was it some collective punishment the Fiend had in mind for the entire Gheet community, as he once had mentioned? Because if so, it honestly was not a well-thought-out plan. The louts upon whom the Fiend so far had snacked were miserable bastards, but they weren't the worst of the Gheets. In fact, those five were the men most responsible for upholding law and order — or what laughingly passed for such in Blenheim County. Gheet thugs might feel license to torment their Surrey neighbors, steal their land and livestock, and butcher their youth, but at least having the law there did something, kept them in check in some minor way.

Not that the situation of her folk could get much worse, but how was the Fiend helping?

She found herself frowning even more deeply.

Deirdre was so deep in thought that she hadn't noticed the murmur of the crowd had softened, and when she did, it occurred to her the frightful sound of steel on steel rang out nearby. With an indifferent sigh, she rose and ambled in that direction. Might as well see how the Fiend intended to put a cap on his most recent shenanigans.

It took Deirdre no time at all to get Isabel undressed and ready for bed. The young woman hadn't exactly celebrated the reverend's "miraculous deliverance" at the duel that day, but she had been so relieved that she'd imbibed far more than she should. Isabel was out like a light, and Deirdre was free to feed her curiosity.

She put the book away, blew out the lamp, and locked the door after leaving the room the two shared. She had a good sense of where the good reverend would be at that moment, and if nothing else had changed in her life, she'd now developed a healthy liking of walking around at night. What was there for her to fear out there?

The duel had gone much as Deirdre had expected. Villeneuve had begun by taunting and toying with the apparently maladroit clergyman until the point when the mayor had tired of his little cat-and-mouse game and moved in for the kill. And then nothing. The reverend, who still pretended to wield his blade clumsily, had parried every blow, cut, and thrust with the barest of success. The mayor, upon whom it slowly had dawned that something terrible was amiss, soon after had fallen into a near panic, and with each increased effort, the silly politician left himself more overextended and more overexposed. To Deirdre's surprise, the parry that severed the arteries in the mayor's neck had looked ungainly yet natural. Even the Fiend had seemed taken aback at how abruptly an otherwise long duel had ended.

Of course, the reverend immediately had fallen to his knees, taken the dying man in arms, and begun to pronounce the last rites. Pure theater.

That spectacle wasn't what she wanted to talk to him about. Nor, in fact, did she want to talk to him about his plans for vengeance. That all still simmered inside of her, and she wanted to think more on the subject and to steady her nerves before seizing that particular bull by the horns. No, there was something else. Something simple and a little silly.

As she entered the cemetery that was situated down the road from the inn, she first detected the telltale and stomach-churning sound she'd expected. The Fiend was at his midnight snack. She stole up to the grave in which earlier that day a large crowd had interred the mayor — the assemblage literally had begged Reverend Ainsley to conduct the ceremony, and he'd undertaken the task with the haggard and haunted face of a man who'd lost his very best friend. Such farce.

She flopped down and leaned against the headstone next to where the Fiend loudly and savagely assailed the mayor's newly exhumed carcass. The sound was like that of a pack of ravenous wolves attacking a fallen elk.

"He wasn't very fat," she observed.

The growling, ripping, and tearing ceased for a moment. "No," said the Fiend in a philosophical tone, "but he was a good fellow and deserves not to go to waste." The ravening resumed.

She almost relented and asked why the man had needed to die, especially if he was a good fellow, but she wasn't ready for that talk, not yet. It ate at her constantly, but she needed to muster her strength. Instead, she yet again rolled her eyes and asked the question she had intended.

"Do you think Isabel is a dullard?" The question, once asked, made her feel dreadful. But it was out in the air now.

The Fiend gave a great swallow. "Isabel? Of course not. She's quite...." There was a pause. "Because she doesn't speak and read proper?"

Deirdre nodded, knowing the Fiend could see her clearly, even in the poor light.

Rather than answering, the Fiend asked an entirely different question. "Have you not been sleeping well?"

She hadn't been, not since Fiona had been so savagely taken, and hot tears stung her eyes. Not thinking about her loss had taken a considerable amount of her waking energy, and though she didn't remember the dreams when each morning she woke, the terror of them haunted her nights.

The Fiend leapt from the grave and soon sat beside her, his arm gently draped across her shoulder. It was obvious from the feel of his clothing and the tenor of his voice that he was Reverend Ainsley again. But when he spoke it wasn't with the reverend's usual pomposity. "Isabel isn't from your world," he said plainly.

What did that mean? "You mean she's from Evaria?" Deirdre had heard of the place but didn't know where it was.

"No, she's from a different world altogether, but one very much like this."

"I don't know what that means."

"Remember what I told you of the two godly tribes? And how each was from a different world? Well, there are many such worlds, so many they are beyond count."

A strange feeling passed over her. "Is Isabel a god?"

"No," was his gentle reply. "She's a person just like you. You see, sometimes the walls between worlds grow weak for no reason, and people tumble through. I think that's what happened to her."

"So, she's not a god?"

"No."

"Or a Gheet?"

"No."

"Oh, thank heavens."

"Isabel is alone in this world, child. She's lost everything and could be a good friend to you, someone you could talk to about your pain."

"I don't...."

"Deirdre, it isn't a cure, but sometimes talking about our pain helps ease it. You need someone like that in your life." For a moment, what sounded like sadness crept into his voice. "It can't be me — I'd only use your pain for my own devices."

His words gave rise to something deep inside her, something that seized her throat and threatened to strangle her. "Am I worth more than three ducats?" she asked in a tearful and trembling voice.

"What...? I...." The Fiend paused and squeezed her shoulder gently. "Child, you are worth all the gold in this and every other world combined, plus two pennies on top. And I'll eat the chitlins of anyone who ever says different."

The girl began laughing amid her tears. It wasn't clear if or how she should voice her thanks, but to her surprise the Fiend's words again had made her feel better. But the smell beside the open grave was getting a bit much. "Speaking of which, the mayor is smelling pretty ripe."

"Well, let's get you back to the inn."

"But what about your dinner?"

The Fiend made a sweet pshaw sound. "Don't worry about that. I already nibbled off the choice bits."

Envy

"To cast a covetous eye on that which is not yours is to curse your neighbor ... and to chart your own course toward damnation."
—**Old High Wols Proverb**

Deirdre endeavored from that moment to befriend Lady Isabel, a stranger in her land, and when next she awoke beside the woman, it was with a smile and a friendly word. It was only when the two went downstairs arm-in-arm that they were greeted by another gift, for they both espied an old friend.

Much to her own amazement, Deirdre squealed like a young girl and ran to throw herself into the arms of Sir Alexis de Vere, who stood outside the common-room door, speaking with the hostler. Lady Isabel soon was beside them, an enormous smile on her face.

"When did you arrive?" the woman asked.

"Before first light," replied the knight. "I'd finished my errand and rushed to see Reverend Ainsley before he departed ... and to see the two of you."

"Where is Reverend Ainsley?" asked a surprised Isabel. "Has he gone?"

Deirdre attempted to feign surprise.

"He was on a nightlong vigil when I found him and didn't want to wake you," said the smiling knight. "But he asked I give you his goodbyes."

Both young ladies made disappointed sounds.

Sir Alexis put a fatherly hand on the shoulder of each. "He did a great kindness for me by looking over the two of you in my absence, delaying a minor pilgrimage he'd promised to undertake when he and I returned from the Holy Land."

"Such a wonderful man," whispered Isabel. "Will we see him again?"

"Oh, you know how the reverend is, Lady Isabel," Deirdre found herself saying. "His body is in this world, but his heart and mind are on the next."

The young woman inhaled. "Sir Alexis, did he tell you of the dreadful thing from just yesterday."

The knight's face took a solemn expression. "No. He spoke not of it, and I didn't ask. But it's talked of up and down the High Road and beyond. These are dreadful and dangerous times, which is why I rushed to rejoin you. There is war in the air."

The two women gasped, and this time Deirdre's was real.

"War?" she was finally able to ask. "War with whom?"

"War among the people," was the knight's sad reply. "Even now I head west to the tournament at Faire Gate to meet cousins of mine. What was to be a celebration of arms, is now to be a conference of peace. Hopefully those assembled will find some solution to the havoc that besets the land." He turned to Isabel, whose eyes had gone wide in fear. "I hope you'll travel with Tuppence and me, m'lady. It's less safe to travel now than it was even a few days past. And your friend Brian Mayfield perhaps will be at the tourney. If not, I'll happily convey you to Mayfield afterward."

The young woman hesitated. "Will … um…?"

"M'lady, I cannot say who may attend the tourney, but while you travel with me, you are under my protection, as if you reside in my very home. None will dare harm or molest you. On this you have my oath."

The kind words of Sir Alexis appeared to ease the lady's fears, and she nodded gratefully. Even Deirdre felt a small knot in her throat at the knight's return. She knew he was the same being as had been with her the day before, but there was something about Sir Alexis, something bracing and reassuring in his bearing. She found herself smiling as she and Isabel went off to their breakfast and the faux knight arranged their travel for the day.

Much to Deirdre's surprise after breakfast, Sir Alexis had completed everything for their departure, including procuring a half dozen riding animals, a pack animal for the various accoutrements he'd obtained, and a pair of war stallions for himself. He'd even obtained the services of a Surrey man he called Birdy to act as groom and helper. In short order, they were on the road and headed west.

Before a quarter of a mile had passed, though, there was a commotion at the graveyard where the day before they'd buried Mayor Villeneuve. Isabel seemed concerned.

Sir Alexis spoke in a woeful tone. "Oh, more villainy in the land, dear lady. Grave robbers. Such riffraff are about whenever a wealthy man is put to rest, looking for jewelry or coin or some other ... choice bits. The lawlessness of late is a calamity."

The Surrey lass resisted yet another urge to roll her eyes, but instead did her utmost to fake a sad smile. But there was another thing. Almost immediately, Deirdre sensed something on the road was amiss, something she'd not felt before, but it was a thing that took her half of the morning to identify.

All who they saw were travelling in large groups, and not just the Surrey — there hardly were any Surrey to be seen — but also the Gheets. And all those people were armed and armored. It neared midmorning when they saw the first flying columns racing by in the distance, and if her nose did not deceive her, there was the smell of smoke in the air. Something was afoot, and though they'd chatted amiably among themselves to that point, Sir Alexis soon instructed that none of them stray from the road and that they all be on their guard.

They were a half-bell past Gatsby when one of the flying columns approached. A group of eight armed and mounted men turned from their course and sped toward the small party. The strangers slowed a hundred yards distant and approached at a walk. It wasn't clear what emboldened them, the fact Deirdre and their friends were so few or the fact that Sir Alexis had the coloration of a Surrey — the Gheet of the north for many years had intermarried with Deirdre's folk — but it was the most foolish stunt imaginable.

After whispering a short command to Birdy, Sir Alexis spurred his horse forward and met the men eighty yards distant. There was what appeared to be a short parlay, after which one of the fools drew a mace and fetched a blow at the head of Sir Alexis, who responded by deflecting the mace, snatching out his sword, and severing the man's arm at the elbow.

Birdy grabbed up the reins of the women's two horses, and the three soon were riding breakneck for a large tree on a small hillock nearby. With Birdy dismounted, a large mace in his hand, Deirdre decided not to be mobile plunder. She stood on her saddle, reached up, and pulled herself into the lower limbs of the enormous elm. She motioned for Lady Isabel to follow, and the two young women were soon twenty or so feet from the ground, watching as Sir Alexis effortlessly thrashed the brigands up one side of the High Road and down the other, like any good knight should.

Lest one of the men escape the knight's vigilance and seek to rob them of their effects, Deirdre called down, "Birdy, keep a close eye on the horses. Lady Isabel and I are safe up here."

"My proper name is actually Charles, miss."

"Birdy, don't be cheeky."

As the Surrey lass leafed through the book she'd brought into the tree with her, she glanced over to a wide-eyed and frightened Lady Isabel on the thick limb next to her. "We're very accustomed to violence in our land," she told the young woman.

Now, she thought, where did I leave off?

———

After the melee near the tree, their travel was far from untroubled, but Isabel had seen the sort of knight who protected them and was able to breathe more freely. She'd always thought of fair Sir Utrecht as a strong and valiant knight — certainly everyone had told her such — but Sir Alexis was a warrior unrivaled. The ease with which he'd driven off the brigands brought to mind the stories of King Arthur and his knights. It was swift and ferocious and so noble that it seemed the knight always gave the enemy a chance to strike the first blow. It availed the fools not.

Several more times during their morning's travels, Birdy stayed back, mace in hand, as Sir Alexis sallied forth and drove off interlopers with the ease by which a wolf might savage a hare. By early afternoon, though, the roads cleared except for larger and better-armed parties, and Isabel realized the tourney must be near. In no time at all, they turned off the road and made for an enormous open field near a babbling stream. It was a sudden glimpse of bucolic ease amid the tumult of the countryside.

Sir Alexis invited her and Tuppence to partake of the festival pavilions that were open nearer to the High Road, but both women stayed close at hand, and they watched as Sir Alexis, Birdy, and some men the knight had engaged erected several tents for their use. The knight dismissed her suggestion that the women might help, and she marveled at the way life went on among the holidaymakers despite the chaos that churned around them.

What was more, the annoyance she'd felt for Tuppence in recent days slowly changed to shame. These folks simply were accustomed to violence and death in ways that the folks of Savannah, Georgia, were not. It was just that simple. The ease with which Tuppence buried her nose in a book was no sign of disregard; It simply was the way things were.

In no time at all, their camp was set, the ladies had refreshed themselves, and Sir Alexis insisted they take advantage of the still-young day and partake of the food, ale, and entertainments of the festival. No one could deny him, and the knight and his two wards soon gently ambled toward the center of the tourney's fairground.

It was delightful. There were amusements of every stripe, people of every type, and contests for folk both lordly and common in anticipation of the next day's festivities. They spent time watching the troubadours, jugglers, archers, and mimes. By late afternoon, the hungry festival-goers had found their way to a broad area about which were cooking fires and food stalls beyond count.

The two ladies reclined at a comfortable bench to sip their ale and partake in a local dish Isabel had come to think of as hummus (she'd forgotten its local name), and Sir Alexis had stepped down the promenade some way to speak with several knights of his acquaintance.

It simply was divine, until the crowd parted, and a man stepped toward the table at which she and Tuppence sat. It was Sir Everett Dupuis, the man who intended to own her.

A woman cried out to her left where Tuppence should have been as Sir Everett grabbed Isabel by the wrist, a gleeful smile on his face, and dragged her into the crowd. The man crowed. He crowed!

"Look here, lads!" he called out to a group who Isabel somehow realized were the man's companions. "Here's my lost bride, laid out for all to see. How could I have misplaced such a gem?"

To her shock and disgust, all present began to laugh, Sir Everett and his louts and others included. Isabel was stunned and unable to speak from the terror. But she felt something warm and comforting at her trembling shoulder as she was dragged like a dog across the fairground, something that slowed her advance to a crawl. It was Tuppence pulling at her. She couldn't see the young woman. But she knew it was her friend. A sudden guilt overwhelmed her. If Tuppence, a girl she scarcely knew and who had befriended her for no reason, could be so brave, so could she.

Sir Everett was incredibly strong, but she pulled against his grip with all her might and cried out. "I'm to be wed to Sir Alexis de Vere! Get your hands from me!"

She'd never thought to say such a thing, and her own words shamed her even more. She'd been raised by a mother who'd taught her a woman was her own person. The humiliation she felt at relying on the name of a man to....

And then Dupuis turned, and the rage and malevolence in his eyes again rendered her mute. At least it did until it occurred to her the look on the man's face was not intended for her, but for someone behind her. Another arm and comforting hand in addition to that of Tuppence gripped her shoulder.

"And I am the happiest man in Albion for it," came the voice of Sir Alexis de Vere. His words were soft and polite. "Now, Sir Everett, be so kind as to unhand the good lady."

―――

What followed was much as Deirdre had come to expect. Sir Alexis was polite beyond words, gently offering Sir Everett his contrite apologies, attempting in ways great and small to make things right between them.

But the more Sir Alexis adopted a position of contrition and friendship, the angrier Sir Everett appeared to grow. Several times, the Gheet knight moved as if he might quit the encounter. But each time, Sir Everett turned again to face Sir Alexis, ever more angry with each passing moment. Deirdre wasn't sure, but it appeared to her that the mildness of Sir Alexis somehow seemed to fuel Dupuis' rage. The whole thing went on for the better part of a quarter bell.

At first, passersby and watchers appeared to take no sides, but over the course of the ever-more voluble encounter (at least voluble on the part of Sir Everett) a number of knights stepped forward to mediate. Several pointed out that Sir Alexis was reaching out his hand in friendship. Why not take it? Sir Everett's constant belligerence began to shift the crowd toward Sir Alexis, until only Dupuis' own followers sided with him.

Somehow, at some point, it grew too much for the angry knight, and on his fourth or fifth move to quit the conversation, he turned about and vigorously struck Sir Alexis across the face.

The thing was done.

The powerful blow scarcely fazed Sir Alexis de Vere, who looked more saddened by the act than angered. But his next words said it all. In a rueful voice, he spoke directly to Sir Everett Dupuis. "I have never owned a blunted sword, sir knight."

Wergild

Those were words of consequence, and several older knights, those foremost among the earlier peacemakers, stepped forward and spoke urgently to Sir Alexis. Deirdre could not hear, but knew the import of them, even her, a commoner. This was not a battle to first blood, nor even until one combatant was unable to continue.

No. This was to be a fight to the death, a thing not uncommon among the gentry, but among the gentry there was no requirement to wait two bells before a duel was to commence. There was no opportunity for cooler heads to prevail. When Deirdre saw the older knights, who whispered with Sir Alexis, nod and raise their palms in acceptance, it was obvious: Sir Everett Dupuis already was a corpse.

She almost felt sorry for the man.

Her first stop was to take an again-distraught Isabel in hand — did folk not duel in her world? After leading the woman to a soft tuft of grass near the tilting field, she spent some time reassuring her that Sir Alexis was the strongest knight in Albion and that the combat between he and the villain Dupuis was a mere formality. It seemed to help a little.

She then repaired to where Birdy helped Sir Alexis don his full armor. There she lounged about, eventually pulling herself up onto the saddle of his warhorse, from where she watched the old fraud prepare for the show. Impatience got the better of her, and she twisted around and squirmed in the saddle as children do, until the knight sent Birdy away to look after Lady Isabel.

"She's going to throw you to the ground, if you're not careful," said the knight, nodding to the great warhorse. As he did, he drew his sword, took a seat on a bench, and began to hone the blade with a whetstone.

Deirdre didn't dismount but instead spun around, arched her back, and lowered her head to regard the now upside-down knight in the upside-down world. "You're not really protecting Lady Isabel's honor, are you?"

"Of course, I am. I'm very fond of her."

"Hmm ... I think she likes you quite a lot, too. But that's not what I mean, and you know it. Sir Everett is on your list, isn't he?"

"Your list," he corrected. "And, yes."

Deirdre reinverted herself and took a proper seat in the saddle. "Okay, if it's my list, when am I getting my vengeance?" Her voice was far more peevish than she'd intended, but it didn't seem to merit an apology.

The knight looked up at her from his chore. Sir Alexis wasn't a handsome man — he was far too hard and rugged for that — but the beautiful smile he cast her now sparkled. "Don't you see it?"

"See what?" Now she was confused.

"Child, war is in the air. Even now bandits and brigands ride the High Road in broad daylight, neighbor turns against neighbor, and the grandees of Blenheim County gather for a moot to devise a solution. The Gheet are reaping the reward of their bad behavior."

"I don't under...," she began. No. The men the Fiend had taken: The magistrate, the sheriff, the bishop, the prosecutor, the mayor, each and every one was a source of order in the county, even if they brought stability for the Gheet and not for the Surrey. "But ... what's to protect...."

"Protect your folk?" asked the Fiend. "You've already said yourself it couldn't get worse for the Surrey folk. And I think you're right. The Gheet did something malignant and blind. They looked the other way while a small portion of them glutted themselves on the blood and property of an unpopular and scorned group of neighbors. I've told you before child, beware of those who enjoy killing too much, because they are the same people who have a hard time telling friend from foe. The attacks on your folk may continue, but the Gheet of this county and beyond now begin to tear at each other in the same way. If Fate is generous and your people find a new courage to fight back, perhaps they can regain some of their rights of old."

She shivered and suddenly was breathless. It was all so magnificent and frightful at the same time. All that blood, all that death. It was her revenge, and she was gripped with an overwhelming urge both to laugh and to cry. But there was something else. She choked back her emotion. "But ... if all this time you've been pushing for war, why has Reverend Ainsley spent the last days preaching peace among the Gheet?"

Sir Alexis turned his blade to sharpen the other side and did a poor job of hiding a smile. "It's a funny thing about preaching," he said in a voice just loud enough for her to hear. "People hear what they hear. The good reverend spent hours preaching about how it is essential to forgive one's neighbors and their trespasses. Did you not see anything strange in that?"

She didn't know how to reply. Wasn't it merely the kind of thing preachers said?

After a half dozen strokes of the stone, the knight rose, sheathed his sword, and stepped over next to her. He looked up at her where she sat on his steed. "In a time when a monster is abroad in the land killing and devouring men whole, why would anyone need to forgive his neighbors?"

It then became obvious to the lass. People always had left the reverend feeling good, buoyant.

As if reading her mind, the knight continued. "Such preaching, demanding forgiveness where none is due, plants the seed of doubt in the human heart, doubt about one's neighbors. And terrified people do horrible, horrible things. The Gheet of this county are now a house divided. Now all they need is a push."

She breathed aloud. "Sir Everett!"

"To start with. He is the king's counselor and an important voice at court. He also is a tax assessor in Blenheim … who has been robbing the king and his subjects blind."

Another breath escaped her. "But wait. That's only six."

"I know," said the knight, now in his full martial regalia. Taking up the reins of the warhorse, he began leading it and Deirdre toward the tilting field, where the combat soon was to commence. "But tomorrow, Baron Sir Etienne de Margot arrives."

The greeting Sir Alexis gave Isabel when he passed by was gentle and reassuring, and he made it perfectly clear that she was bound to him in no way. This combat was a matter of honor between him and Everett Dupuis. He then led the steed, with Deirdre still astride, to the mark where the knights were to meet.

"She's sweet on you," said Deirdre once they were out of earshot.

The knight, his eyes clearly visible beneath the helm's faceplate, gave her a wink. "What's not to love?"

When they reached their mark, she made to scamper from the saddle. The youngster was still far from an expert rider, and she was very high off the ground. After several futile attempts to dismount, she felt herself lifted to the ground, and the knight gave her a gentle swat on the bottom to send her on her way. It wasn't until she reached Isabel and Birdy that she realized there was a gaping smile on her face. The whole affair suddenly was feeling too much like a carnival to her, so she bit her lip and put her arms around Lady Isabel.

"Sir Alexis is the strongest knight in Albion," she repeated by way of excuse for her high spirits. "You have nothing to fret about. He'll make short work of this bloke."

"Tuppence," said the woman in a voice that trembled, "they say the same of Sir...." The woman cut off her words and tears again streamed from her eyes.

Deirdre managed to comfort the woman in a convincing way, and the duel was soon commenced.

Sir Alexis did not make a liar of her. Unlike the reverend's duel with the mayor, the battle between the mounted knights lasted but one pass of their steeds. The men exchanged but three sword-blows each, and Sir Everett toppled from his mount, attempted to rise several times, and gripped his neck in despair. His throat had been cut cleanly through by one of the blows delivered expertly by Sir Alexis. There was a shocked silence at the abruptness and finality of the combat. Sir Alexis dismounted, knelt by the fallen knight, and whispered briefly in his ear. The fallen man soon afterward was dead.

"The thing is decided," cried out the old knight who had acted as marshal. "Honor has been satisfied."

And it was over.

Rather than rejoice, it looked as if Lady Isabel might faint. Heavens, she was a strange woman. Deirdre pampered her and, with Birdy's aid, took her back to their tent for a rest. When the lass emerged, Sir Alexis was stretched in the grass, his armor and arms in a neat pile where Birdy had placed them before tottering off to enjoy the festival. Sir Alexis was a liberal master.

She flopped down in the grass beside the creature she knew to be a faux knight, but she couldn't escape the special feeling she had around Sir Alexis. It was like he and Reverend Ainsley were different creatures entirely, even though she knew they were not. The former was ... she couldn't put her finger on it. He somehow was purer and more decent, even when it was just the two of them alone. The reverend was the consummate actor, but from time to time, even in public, his mask would slip a fraction and the real Fiend beneath would flash a grin. Not so with the mighty knight.

"What did you whisper to Sir Everett just before he died," she asked the knight after a comfortable silence.

"I told him I was going to dig him up tonight and eat his innards."

Wergild

For just a moment, Deirdre was struck dumb. "You're teasing me," she said at last. Maybe his mask did slip sometimes.

"I tease not."

"Why ... why would you do that?"

"He was a monstrous man, Tuppence, cruel and vicious. The world is a better place without him."

"And the wind told you this, too?"

"After a fashion. Sir Alexis knew him of old in the Holy Land. Dupuis was malevolent and rapacious there as well."

She again was speechless, but it then dawned on her Sir Alexis previously had mentioned knowing the man, and some of the words that had passed earlier that day between Sir Alexis and Dupuis had hinted at an existing familiarity. It simply wasn't something that she'd connected at the time. "So ... there is an Alexis de Vere?"

"There was," he replied with a nod. "He died ... drowned crossing the channel about four days before you met him near Portsmouth."

She couldn't help but smile. "And was there a Right Reverend Moorcroft Ainsley?"

"Oh, no. He's a creature of pure wind."

"I'll say," she laughed. "So, when you said you were to meet cousins here, that wasn't a lark? Sir Alexis does have cousins?"

"Indeed, he does. And good folk, too. You'll meet them tomorrow."

The knowledge that the knight had family tickled her, and it dawned on Deirdre that she too might be a bit sweet on Sir Alexis, at least the idea of him. "What was he really like?"

He gave her a look she'd not yet seen and flicked away a few innocent blades of grass. "Do you know what it is for a person to change, Tuppence? And I mean to *truly* change?"

She shook her head.

"When Alexis de Vere was a young knight, he was the very model of everything you despise in a Gheet — cruel, selfish, quick to anger, slow to forgive ... belligerent and spiteful even to those closest to him. But fifteen years ago, he went to the Holy Land, and something happened to him there. I can't fully say what — the wind doesn't tell me everything — but somehow, he looked inside himself and took a careful accounting of what he saw. And he made himself a better person." The Fiend gave his head a gentle shake. "People almost never change, Tuppence. But sometimes they do."

"You're not gonna be eating chitlins wearing his face, are you?" she whispered.

"I would never."

"Good." The whole idea of Sir Alexis brought a smile to her face on an otherwise complex and disorienting day. But something again dawned on her. "Wait, is that what the reverend said to Mayor Villeneuve?"

"What? About the chitlins?"

She nodded.

"No, Reverend Ainsley begged the mayor's pardon, swore there was nothing between he and Mrs. Villeneuve, and pleaded to give him last rites, to which the man consented."

Now the young woman was confused, even more than before. She made several incoherent noises as she tried to speak.

The knight continued speaking. "He wasn't a bad man, Tuppence … not like the others. There *are* good people in the world. You just don't find many in government."

"But … you *did* eat his …."

"He wasn't using them anymore," the Fiend protested in a mild voice.

"But … okay." It took her another moment to sort her thoughts. "Okay, if he was such a great guy, why did you roger his wife? And don't you dare say you were in the chapel speaking in tongues."

For just the barest moment a look of embarrassment flashed over the manly face of Sir Alexis, Fiend incognito. "Okay, I needed to do that to get the man's attention."

"Bullshit."

"Tuppence…."

"I don't believe you," was her flat reply. "You had no problem getting the attention of the others upon whom you wanted to pounce…." The thought hit her like a limb crashing from a tree. "You needed him to challenge you. Why? ... *In the same way you needed Sir Everett to challenge you!"*

Another nigh imperceptible look flashed across the knight's strong face, this one a look of deep surprise. It was gone in an instant. "You are very clever," he said in the most affectionate of tones.

She'd found out something about him, something important. "Why did they need to challenge you? Why didn't…?" It all opened up before her as if the dawn had just broken. In all her time with him, the Fiend had not picked a single fight or cast a single first blow. He'd never goaded, he'd never challenged, and he'd never struck first. He was sweetness and probity incarnate until his victims struck the first blow. What was going on? "Baron de Margot," she whispered.

"What of him?"

"You were trying to pick a fight with him at the inn that night, at the Four Quarters."

The knight laughed aloud, before continuing in a low voice. "And if it hadn't been for that fat amiable dolt Armand de Bois-Guilbert, insufferable peacemaker that he is, I wouldn't have been so hungry the next evening when I supped on Magistrate Servais."

"So, he *is* the seventh?"

The knight nodded. "De Margot? I hoped he'd be the first, but it still works out well. I'll have another chance tomorrow."

"How so?"

"There is to be a moot, tomorrow. It wasn't originally part of the tourney. But the nobles gather to seek peace. The wind tells me de Margot will attend. He must."

"And you'll convince him to challenge you?"

The Fiend smiled and shrugged. "Dupuis and he were close. He'll want vengeance for that, especially since Dupuis' death ruins schemes the two had together. De Margot is an ambitious man. Though the moot is a place of peace, he'll dig for some reason to shame me, accuse me of all manner of sins in doing so. Ask Lady Isabel. That's his way of picking fights, by shaming men into challenging him."

"But you won't fall for that?"

Alexis began to laugh aloud. "Of course not, Tuppence. That's my trick. I won't let that rascal steal it from me."

Deirdre needed to cover her mouth to keep from crying out in laughter. "Why?" she asked after she composed herself. "Why must your enemies cast the first blow?"

"It's the way of things, Tuppence — it's sort of a loophole. I can't explain it any other way."

"So," she continued slowly, "you can't kill someone until they strike you first?"

"It isn't a great impediment, child. You know better than most the Gheet are a proud and violent people … and terribly easy to provoke." He gave a chuckle. "It's a peculiarity of human nature, at least among the male gender, that mildness and pleas for amity often incite the greatest rage."

She found herself laughing again, and they continued to joke and laugh throughout the afternoon. After a while, Lady Isabel awoke and joined them, and soon after, Birdy returned. They ate and drank and laughed, the four of them, well into the evening.

Later, as Deirdre prepared for sleep, she had time to think and ponder the odd and strange Fiend who she'd befriended — for she realized now they truly were friends. And though she had not been perfectly convinced until that afternoon that the Fiend might not yet eat her, she knew now he never would. The thought enabled her to sleep better, even if only a little better, than she had in some time.

Pride

"Scripture tells us that Pride is the sin of the Devil, that deep and irreparable flaw that makes Him what He is."
— **Right Reverend Moorcroft Ainsley**

Isabel awoke to the sounds of hammers striking blows on wood — tents were being erected nearby — but soon after, the shouts of anger began. It was such a common sound in this land that she tried not to panic, but she swiftly dressed and stepped outside the tent. Beyond the flap, she found Tuppence and Birdy watching a knot of armed men riding toward the tourney's main field. At their head was Sir Alexis de Vere.

"What's going on?" she asked her friend when she reached the girl's shoulder. "Where's Sir Alexis off to?"

Tuppence gave one of her inscrutable looks. "A wild animal dug up and devoured Sir Everett's body last night. His cousin, the Baron de Margot arrives even now." The young girl put her arm around Isabel in an awkward attempt to comfort her. "There may be a fight."

Isabel steadied herself. That was always the way in this benighted land. It was dreadful and hateful, but there was no other choice than to trust to Sir Alexis.

Tuppence, strong, tough, unflappable Tuppence, snatched up her hand and began to lead her in the direction the knights had ridden, before calling back, "Birdy, stay here and watch the tents."

It was less than a ten-minute walk, but it took some minutes more before the young women could find a place to watch among the throng. With just a bit of pushing and wiggling, they soon were within a dozen yards of Sir Alexis, who stood tall amid a group of men who had gathered in a shallow depression below. The armed men were several hundred and stood around an opening about thirty yards in diameter.

On the far side of the circle, a commotion drew Isabel's eye, and she looked to see Etienne de Margot step through an opening in the crowd. She felt her body shiver and her hand shift to the hilt of the dagger Tuppence had gifted her. The man's brow was knitted, and a look of deep fury etched his face. He was a dreadful sight, but no less so than was the chortling rogue who had killed Sir Utrecht.

"This is the moot!" heralded a deep baritone. The voice was that of a lean old knight who appeared to have mounted some sort of platform twenty or so feet distant. "All speak in peace. All speak the truth."

The assembled knights murmured the same words in return, and all made gestures with their hands Isabel had not seen before. Clearly, some sort of oath had been invoked. Before the old knight said a word more, Sir Alexis stepped forward and ascended the podium.

"I would speak," said her protector in a deep and powerful voice.

The overall din fell, but across the way several outraged voices were raised. Baron de Margot veritably trembled with rage. "What have you to say then, de Vere?" he cried out in a voice that was thick with fury. "We are here for the moot, not your prideful arrogance! All know of your hunger for power, your lust for what's not yours!"

Sir Alexis appeared to ignore the man, and he again raised his voice. "By right, I would speak."

The din fell even more, but the crowd across the ground, that bunch nearest de Margot, continued to mutter and to give ugly looks. Baron de Margot again appeared as if he might speak before being forestalled.

"This is a place of peace," cried a voice that Isabel thought to be the older knight who first had spoken. "Baron de Vere has claimed his right!"

Baron? Isabel looked over at Tuppence, who returned her look with one of equal surprise. There then was a moment's silence upon the ground, and the voice of Alexis de Vere covered all.

"You know me of old, Sir Emil Severance," he said, pointing to a large bearded knight nearby.

"Aye," the man agreed. "I know you, Baron Alexis."

"And you, Sir Dewald Avery."

"Aye, baron. I know you."

Sir Alexis named a half dozen other knights, most of them older, and each acknowledged his acquaintance. The noise around Baron de Margot grew with each passing moment.

Baron de Vere did not deign to notice them, but continued. "I was the worst of men in my youth...."

"You'll get no argument from Sir Everett," sneered a voice from near de Margot.

Wergild

"The worst to my friends, the worst to my neighbors, the worst to those most beloved of me...."

This time de Margot, in a gloating tone, spoke up himself. "My cousin who you slew and who knew you well in the Holy Land could have spoken well to that, de Vere. You were the most covetous and hungry of...."

The voice of Alexis de Vere grew to an unnatural strength and volume. "I was all those things in my youth, Baron de Margot. I need no witness or jury. I was the *worst* of men. And in my absence from this fair land, my beloved cousin William, who I slandered and wronged all those years ago, a man I wronged in every way a man can wrong another, has behaved toward me better than any brother ever could ask. In my absence, he has tended my affairs, collected my rents, spoken in my name, and fought my fights ... with never once seeking thanks or recompense." Alexis looked straight to de Margot, who again seemed about to speak. "You know well the love of a cousin, Baron de Margot. This I know."

The candor of Alexis de Vere's words seemed to shock de Margot, who for that moment was struck silent.

Sir Alexis raised a rolled parchment above his head, one that Isabel had not before noticed. "Everything I own, I own through Fleming Law, passed to me not through the crown, but through my own family right. By this charter, I hereby give everything I own of worth to my cousin Sir William de Vere, formerly Baron of Flight, now Baron of Flight and Inskeep. All of my lands, all of my titles, all of my fields, all of my flocks, all I own but my horse, armor, and arms are his, now and forever after. I swear this. Do you witness this, Sir Emil Severance?"

"I witness it, Sir Alexis."

"Do you witness this, Sir Dewald Avery?"

Sir Alexis continued his query until each of the knights he originally had named had sworn and attested they were witnesses to the grant.

And then it appeared the thing was done, but Isabel didn't know exactly what had transpired, save that it was a thing of import and great nobility. She looked to Tuppence, but the lass merely shrugged her shoulders, a confused look on her face that no doubt mirrored Isabel's own.

The moot went on, with knights stepping forward and speaking their grievances over recent events. There was a fair amount of hollering and some angry shouting, as well as many ayes and nays, but a now spellbound Isabel was focused on Sir Alexis. Something was afoot, and she knew not what. Her protector was deep in conversation with a man who could only be his cousin. The two men grasped each other firmly at the forearm and spoke in low and candid tones. After several minutes, Sir Alexis raised his eyes and met hers. A smile broke across his face, and he waved her and Tuppence toward him.

With Tuppence by her side, Isabel approached the two men with her heart rising in her throat and a broad smile on her face. When they reached Sir Alexis, the man spoke.

"Cousin," he said, "this is my ward Lady Deirdre, who humors me by allowing me to call her Tuppence. And this is Lady Isabel, who travels under my protection and who I also would take as ward if she so seeks it. I ask only one boon of you, that if anything ever should befall me that you take these young ladies in as your own wards and look after them as if they were your own kin."

"Oh, happily." Baron William's words were warm and threaded with emotion. "They are evermore welcome in my home as friends *and* family, no matter what comes."

Isabel felt happy tears form in her eyes and found herself nodding wordlessly as the baron, who very much resembled Sir Alexis, save younger and more slender, looked Lady Isabel and Tuppence — no, Lady Deirdre — in the eye, each in turn. "You ladies are my kin now," was all he said to them.

The two men then embraced and chatted some moments more about topics Isabel understood not, and then came the voice she'd dreaded to hear.

"And what of *my* cousin!" Sir Etienne de Margot nearly screamed aloud. "Murdered by a scoundrel and his noble body left for the wolves to harry! Is this the type of man you are, Baron de Vere?"

Alexis de Vere's reply was loud, but even and tempered. "My cousin is the Baron de Vere, sir knight, and he has just this morning arrived, as have you. Your beloved cousin in his haste offered me up an insult and a challenge that could not be refused, and he was killed in honorable combat...."

De Margot nearly screamed and was only stopped from attacking Sir Alexis by an enormous knight beside him. The sounds that erupted from de Margot were more animal than human, and over those feral shrieks, Sir Alexis again spoke, his voice stern and insistent.

"In honorable combat, sir, as witnessed by more than one-hundred knights, including your cousin's own comrades." Alexis raised his voice further in the face of de Margot's rage. "And none here are at fault but Sir Everett's own retainers and men-at-arms for not standing vigil over his body at a time when...."

By that time, Etienne de Margot was a man out of control. Isabel's heart raced at what would happen next, for when it came, it was shocking and sudden. From nowhere, de Margot produced a dagger, turned, and slashed at the small party of his own men who restrained him. His eyes filled with murder and weapon in hand, the man lunged at Sir Alexis.

Deirdre grabbed Isabel and hauled her up the rise to a spot behind the nearest clump of trees. She'd seen bloodlust in men, and neither of the women were safe at that moment as the moot dissolved into a scene of anarchy. The key now was to keep quiet and keep out of sight. Men in a battle-rage could do most anything.

Still, she bit her lip to keep from laughing aloud. It was the Fiend, all the Fiend. Something in her exulted even as another part cringed.

Several times she caught sight of Sir Alexis amid the churning scrum in the field below, swinging his sword in powerful overhand strokes and shoving and kicking men aside. She was not the least worried for him, but he and his cousin, Baron William, were in the worst of it. All of the men were armed, but none were wearing armor beyond a chainmail byrnie or hauberk. Some few had little more than a leather doublet to protect them.

Glancing about to try and discern the location of Baron William, she saw an enormous form dragging itself arm-over-arm from the press. The massive bulk was that of Armand de Bois-Guilbert, the great dolt of whom Sir Alexis had spoken so fondly. The poor wretch had been cut down by his own liege lord as he again had tried to dissuade de Margot from violence, from breaking the sacred peace of the moot.

Peacemaker. Ha.

But cut down by his own lord? She wanted to ignore the man — he was just a Gheet, and a knight at that — but a will other than her own propelled her down the rise to where the man struggled.

She soon felt another form beside her, and then a third. She, Isabel, and a newly-arrived Birdy dragged the gargantuan warrior, who was more muscle than fat, but weighed like a year-old ox, back to their hiding place amid the trees. As Birdy watched over them with his mace in hand, she and Isabel nursed the silly and valiant oaf, who was bleeding dreadfully from a deep laceration to his neck. She hoped she was doing the right thing by helping the man, but it didn't matter. She couldn't persuade herself to do anything different.

The melee was over nearly as quickly as it had begun, and soon the survivors were sifting through the mess trying to find family, friends, and fallen comrades. Before she knew it, they were back at the tents of Baron William, Sir Armand with them.

For all her many shortcomings around violence, Lady Isabel was a whirlwind as a healer, and she soon was giving orders, demanding pure alcohol and boiled water, and insisting on how the wounded were to be treated. Deirdre helped as she was able, but in less than a quarter bell she found herself getting in the way and went outside to find Sir Alexis. It took her some minutes to spy him on a nearby hilltop, where he was looking off to the east.

As she approached him, she already could hear the din in the distance, the noises of flight, pain, and terror. When she crested the rise and stood next to the ersatz knight, the panorama before them was anarchy, complete pandemonium. Billows of smoke from fully a dozen fires were visible in the distance, refugees clogged the roads, and squadrons of knights and men-at-arms rode here and yon. It was a bloody hellscape.

The Fiend raised his arms before him, palms heavenward, like an artist regarding a favored portrait. "This is my finest work, Tuppence, my masterpiece. And I couldn't have done any of it without you."

Without her? A thrill ran through the lass, an ethereal something that told her the Fiend referred to more than just their agreement. She couldn't put it into words. But it was clear that all of this was in some way her doing. More, there was something the Fiend hadn't told her, something about him that she should have seen from the beginning. It dawned on her now like the rising sun.

She wanted to speak, to cry out loud of her discovery. But for the moment, her prudence and caution got the better of her raw excitement, and she instead pointed to the moot ground. "What happened down there?"

"More than I ever could've dreamed. I knew de Margot schemed with Dupuis to skim tax money headed for the crown — and evidence of that will be made public soon — but I hadn't realized the extent of his plans until he arrived. He is a powerful and rich man, and with Dupuis' help, he intended to land a place at court. The king is weak, and in a few years, he may have usurped him."

Wergild

"Again," she asked patiently, still concealing her excitement, "what happened?"

He looked down at her and smiled, and when he did, he draped an arm over her shoulder and pulled her close. "Neither of the de Vere baronies were especially large, but when I ceded to cousin William all I owned, that made William the single largest and richest landholder in Albion. William now has great tracts of land, castles, fortified towns, and control of the second largest port in the country. He even has lands here in the south. When de Margot realized that, he snapped. Everything he'd planned since arriving from Ghitland a dozen years ago went up in smoke." The Fiend began to chuckle.

Deirdre finally gave up hiding her glee and laughed with him. "Are you eating his chitlins, tonight?"

"Mmm ... no. I thought it best to let him go for a time." He forestalled her protest. "I'll get to him someday, soon — maybe Reverend Ainsley will take his confession. But until then, he'll be a source of conflict. When the king finds out of his plotting, de Margot will have to raise arms against him. Likely William and other barons will side with the crown, but the war between them will be long and bloody, and your people...."

"If they are brave and strong...." She left the rest unsaid.

"If they are brave and strong," he repeated. "I can't predict the future, Deirdre. But now your folk have a chance." He gave her a squeeze. "Speaking of courage, I'm proud of what you did to help Sir Armand. You have an enormous heart, and you helped him even without knowing it was to our advantage to do so."

She shook her head in confusion, and the Fiend continued speaking.

"Armand is a great and lovable oaf, but he's also honest and is admired after a fashion. When he tells his tale of de Margot's cutting him down, cutting his own men, and breaking the peace of the moot, people will believe him."

She looked up at him. "What are we to do now?"

"Hmm...?" He glanced down. "Don't you want to return to your home?"

"I can't," Deirdre whispered. "I cursed my parents before I left. I cursed everyone. Besides, you and I have a deal."

The Fiend ignored her last words. "Families can be understanding, far more understanding than we sometimes imagine."

She shook her head again. The Fiend knew so much, but he didn't know this.

But she knew something and realized it was time. She braced herself. After three long breaths, she asked the question that had occurred to her only moments before. "You're not really just a Fiend, are you?"

Sir Alexis said nothing and gave only a wispy smile as Deirdre continued.

"But you're not the Walking God, either ... are you? For just a moment, I thought you might be, but ... no. You're the Other One."

He again looked down with an affectionate smile. "Bards, priests, and poets, they so often mix up our stories, his and mine. I should have known you'd puzzle it out, Tuppence. But whatever you do, don't tell Lady Isabel. The folk of her world are even more afraid of my kind than are the people of this one."

To Deirdre's shock and amazement, the counterfeit knight's revelation didn't frighten her, not in the least. It was a complete mystery why — she should have been petrified.

"How...." But neither did she know what to ask. Her lips moved several times without making a sound.

It took him only moments to show her charity.

"The difference between me and this Walking God of yours is *not* about good and evil. It's about ...," he shook his head gently several times as he often did, "... it's about the difference between servitude and freedom ... what some fools might call order and chaos."

"And you're chaos?"

"Tuppence, you know the answer to that better than anyone." He again chuckled. "No. I cannot claim perfection, far from it. I am of a tribe that believes that a world in which folks have freedom to choose their own paths will be a world happiest for all."

"But only if they're strong?"

"Yes, if they strive to make their lot better," he said with a nod. "Because otherwise, what's the choice? The cold, dead, and miserable hand of the law, of rules and regulations — of tyrants and kings?"

He turned to meet her gaze, his hand still resting gently on her shoulder.

"Tuppence, my people have one thing that the other godly tribe will never own: We know what it is to care, fully and irrationally, for someone other than ourselves. We know what it is to hold friendship in esteem, to value loyalty — and we know what it is to love. That other creature that was left on this world with me, that so-called Walking God, sits in a marble palace even now in Etruscia and does *nothing* but adheres to the rules, no matter how damnable. If the rules required that he dice up his own mother and chuck her in the cooking pot for stew, he would do so without hesitation and then rush back to his salon with nary a thought of it after. Is that any sort of world worth living in?" Her companion again shook his head. "They call us evil, but I would never do harm to anyone I love. *Ever.* I'd burn this universe to a cinder first, and if that makes me evil, then it's a brand I'll wear proudly."

Deirdre felt a deep warmth run through her, but she had to ask, to hear it with her own ears. "Then you're not ever gonna eat my chitlins?"

The smiling knight, his eyes glossy with emotion, delivered a tender kiss to her forehead. "Sweet Tuppence, as long as I have a body to shield you, no harm will ever come to you."

For just a fleeting moment, the screaming rage that had seized her those many weeks past abated, and an enormous wave of relief washed over her. This was what she needed — it was all anyone really ever needed — one person, just one person who was in her corner, one person who always would be in her corner, come what may.

What did it matter if that one person for her just happened to be the Devil?

The End

Made in the USA
Monee, IL
20 June 2024